I have been an avid reader ever since I was young, and I have always loved the freedom that a good book can offer to a reader; the chance to immerse your imagination into something entirely different, the chance to open up new realms of fantasy, all made possible with the combination of words and your own mind.

From about the age of seven, I could often be found with my head in a book written by Roald Dahl or Rudyard Kipling. As I grew, my passion for reading increased, and I found myself pursuing new authors and genres.

By the time I had reached the age of about fifteen, I had pretty much read something from every categories that literature had to offer, my taste had been pretty much whittled down to two genres: horror and thrillers.

I have found that these two categories aren't mutually exclusive. Some thrillers walk a fine line between stepping into the horror genre and vice versa. Let's not forgot some of the violent, horrific scenes that Lee Child offered up in the first of his Jack Reacher novels – *Killing Floor*, or the Jack Daniels series that were written by J.A Konrath, both perfect examples of how taut thrillers can edge into the shady realms of horror. There is always a protagonist and there is always someone who is their adversary looking to catch them.

When I first started writing, I was concentrating strictly on horror. I have a keen understanding and adept mind for the construction process that goes into a horror story. As I continued to write, that little voice inside my mind was screaming out for me to create the concept for an idea, one that had been milling about in the archives of my mind for a while.

That concept was to become the basis for *Bound*.

I had all of the details already mapped out in my

mind; it was a simple matter of execution. However, I was missing one key element, one thing was missing to try and pull off the idea that would make the story a little different. It eventually came to me; to use a second writer.

I approached Andrew Lennon. Initially he was a little tentative as he was unsure of the genre, and it was looking to take him completely out of his comfort zone – this was something that I encouraged. I wanted to push him, I wanted to make him uncomfortable, and in most cases, I'm glad to say that I was successful.

So, how did we go about writing the book? My initial thought was to do a split narrative between the good guy and the bad guy, with one of us writing from the aspect of one character each. After discussing this with Lennon, we decided that were going to try something a little different. Where both of us would be using all of the elements of the plot and characters. I was to start the process, and fire the story over to him, leaving it at a part of the story for him to continue in his own style. Once his next section was complete he would send it back to me to continue and vice versa. At no point did we discuss what each of our respective parts would contain. We both agreed that we could go with anything that we felt would work, as long as it was befitting to the overall structure of the concept.

I would like to think it was a success. We worked hard to try and make the book as elaborate as possible, whilst not losing the main focus; enjoyment for the reader. So, here we have it, *Bound*. Strap yourself in and I hope you enjoy the ride.

Matt Hickman

Extract from the Manchester Gazette 17th July,

2013

Detective Chief Inspector Mark Gunn of the Greater Manchester Police has confirmed that early this morning, the dead body of a woman in her mid-twenties was discovered in a derelict industrial building in the Salford region of the city. At this stage, he was unable to comment on whether the death has any relation to the murders of three other women within the past six months, from various locations around the City Centre.

February 2013

Lucy French

Lucy entered the Starbucks coffee shop and ordered herself a tall Latte. She paid and collected her drink from the end of the counter. Choosing a table nearest the window, she placed her various bags of shopping beneath the table, and sat in the high chair next to the large pane of glass that overlooked the street. She stared at the picturesque landscape; a brisk winter's day, despite the sun beaming low in the sky, where the breeze was fresh and particularly cold.

Outside, from within a parked car, a camera shutter flickered.

It had been a long morning. She had agreed to meet her friend in the coffee house at midday. She decided that, beforehand, she would treat herself to a little retail therapy. Her husband had a decent income, the couple had no children to squander his salary on, thus he rarely cared when she put a dent in the credit card balance.

A shrill noise emanated from inside her designer handbag. She grabbed her mobile phone and clicked the button to unlock it. A text message was waiting for her from a friend, stating that she was running a little late. She would be there in about ten minutes. Looking at the time on her phone it displayed, 11:54 a.m.

Using the touch screen on the device, she quickly tapped a message back to her friend, confirming that it wasn't a problem, and tossed the phone back into her handbag.

She took a sip of the fresh coffee; the heat of the liquid burned her lips and the harsh, bitter taste made her wince. It was a good, strong brew.

Looking around the place, there were only a

handful of customers – it was still a little early for the lunchtime rush. An elderly couple sat at a table next to her, quietly chatting about the previous evening's television highlights. A woman dressed in a sharp black suit, suitable for the office, sat quietly by a table at the other end of the room, gently stroking at the keys of her laptop, most likely preparing a sales forecast or business report. Perched on a stool at one of the raised tables, a large, middle-aged man was chewing the end of his pen thoughtfully whilst filling out the answers to the daily crossword in his newspaper. In the seats to his left, two young men were having a discussion and sharing friendly banter about football.

She leaned forward in her chair, letting her hands gently caress the taut muscles in her thighs, and then moved down to her calves. Although she was only a slim, twenty-nine year old, her morning had consisted of three solid hours of marching in and out of designer stores at the shopping centre. This type of intensive retail assignment could match that of a military boot camp.

Outside, from within a parked car, a camera shutter flickered.

Lucy reached for her handbag again. Unfastening the clip, she rooted around the collection of junk inside and grabbed a small make up mirror. Gazing at her reflection, she checked her make up - it looked freshly applied, her hair tied back in an obligatory ponytail, not obscuring her face as she checked her reflection in the mirror.

Despite her relatively young age, she had started to see one or two little creases beginning to sneak into the corners of her cheeks, and small crow's feet were starting to form at the sides of her eyes. Speckles of grey had begun to creep into her once mousy blonde hair, and she could feel the remnants of a second chin beginning to appear. She hardly found it surprising, even to herself, since she had no need to work. She worked out regularly, but she heard that wasn't enough nowadays, diet mattered too, so she expected to gain a little weight on the way to her thirties. Her husband saw to the finances, and she had no responsibilities or dependents, no children to worry or stress about, but she enjoyed their lavish, independent lifestyle. It came at a price, however.

Sometimes, life was just a bitch.

Placing the mirror back into the bag, she grabbed and checked the time on her mobile phone; it now read 12:03 p.m. She tossed the handset back into the bag and placed it onto the floor, below the table. She took another swig from her coffee, savouring the gentle aroma and the rich taste.

A few minutes passed as Lucy leaned back in her chair, staring out of the window. The volume of traffic steadily increased as office workers and other commuters began to head into town for the beginning of their lunch breaks.

Lucy was delighted as she heard her friend's familiar voice; it broke the air with a cheerful greeting. Turning and standing up from her chair, the two women gave each other a quick kiss on each cheek, and a brief hug. Lucy offered to buy her friend a drink. Once she had placed her order and paid, both women sat down at their table and began to chat away happily.

Outside, from within a parked car, a camera shutter flickered.

March 2013

Vicky Stuart

Outside of work, John didn't have much of a life. Friday night. The nightclub was absolutely heaving with excited punters. Dry ice rose from the sticky dance floor, the mist forced into the surrounding areas, corridors and numerous bars. People were bouncing away rhythmically to the sound of the loud music. Cheers arose from the appreciative crowd, as the DJ mixed one tune into another seamlessly. Lights and lasers spun and flickered, twisting and turning, throwing shapes and illuminations across the walls and floors. The thunderous bass continued to thump from the clubs innovative sound system, shaking the room.

She stood amongst the crowd, swaying among the masses of people, her arms held high above her head, lithe fingers outstretched and reaching for the lasers. Her body was in a trance-like state of euphoria; she felt elation like never before.

It had been a little over an hour since she'd taken the small white tablet, and washed it down with cool water. She managed to purchase it from one of the unregulated dealers inside the nightclub. At twenty-six years old, it was the first time she'd ever taken drugs. The serotonin slowly released from her brain, increased by the MDMA she had taken; it gave her the feeling of utmost relaxation, confidence and an overwhelming sensation of empathy. She was happily speaking to strangers and exchanging appreciative nods and hugs. Although these people *were* strangers, in that moment, they felt like real friends. Old friends.

She had no objection to drug use; she'd always

taken a liberal stance on most subjects, but tonight was about making a fresh start. Her decision was final, regardless of anyone else, and his or her opinions - it was time for her to start looking after number one for a change.

She continued to dance. All that mattered, right here and right now, was the sound of the music, alive and energetic as it thundered around in her mind. She had never felt this serene in her entire life.

All around the large club, she could sense the same feeling; a feeling of unity, bonding and, albeit chemically induced, mutual love.

Vicky was a pretty girl; her straight brown hair fell to the middle of her face. She had stunning natural features, striking blue eyes, firm, smooth lips, and a perfect complexion – a girl that benefited from natural beauty, a girl that rarely needed to wear makeup.

Thirty minutes passed in what seemed to be a few seconds. Vicky realised that she needed a drink. The nightclub was stifling hot, the lack of air conditioning combined with the number of people crammed into such a small space made it sweaty and claustrophobic.

Not that she minded the unity.

Walking from the dance floor, she headed in the direction of the main bar, a little unsteady on her feet due to the chemicals washing around her nervous system. Standing in the queue, she turned and looked around. It was mind blowing; she had never seen so many people in such a small amount of space. Everywhere, people were dancing, sat at tables, drinking and attempting to speak above the ridiculous volume of the music, their heads bent low. A particularly excitable couple next to her at the bar were engaged in a heavy tonguing session, groping at each other greedily. She looked away with a wry smile.

Vicky looked above, her dilated eyes roaming to the high ceiling – a vast glass construction above the dancefloor, a unique element that added another dimension to the drug-fuelled proceedings. She could see people walking across it, staggering in some cases, their feet pushed against the solid surface. A drink spilled, splattering and sliding across the transparent floor space like some kind of abstract art. Vicky smiled, remembering the sign at the entrance. *The Loft – Manchester's Premier Night Spot To Get Sky High.*

They weren't kidding.

As she glanced at the glass, through it, to the busy club above, she felt a little giddy, euphoric. There was no feeling like it. The drugs elevated the design to levels beyond her comprehension. It was truly unique.

Turning as the barman handed the last punter their change, she shouted in his direction, ordering a fresh bottle of water. Returning, the barman handed over the drink as she paid. Unscrewing the lid, she took a deep, long swig. The cold contents sluiced downwards and hit her stomach, going right through her, giving Vicky the urge to use the bathroom.

The female toilets were disgusting. Each of the sinks were overflowing with dirty water, and pooling onto the floor. The putrid stench of stale urine, combined with overpowering perfume, hung in the air. Glancing over into one of the cubicles, she spotted a clogged lavatory, blocked with toilet paper and overflowing with dirty, brown water. Standing at the mirrors, women were re-applying make-up or brushing their hair. Small groups had gathered and were discussing the events of the evening, commenting on the amount of talent in the club.

As she passed by one of the groups, a woman made eye contact and pleasantly smiled in acknowledgment. She returned the look with a sheepish smile, before heading towards the cubicle at the end of the row. She hitched up her skirt, and pulled her cotton knickers down to her ankles, being careful not to let them become soaked in the spilled water. Whilst sitting, she heard a muffled conversation between two women in the next cubicle; a discussion about cutting up lines of cocaine. Figuring that this was normal clubbing culture, and something that she would have to get used to, she ignored the discussion and went back into her own trance.

She sat staring at the back of the cubicle door, the pleasant caress of the chemicals flowing through her body felt amazing. Her vision kept blurring slightly, and then dropping back into focus. It felt strange but nice. She smiled.

Once done, she exited the cubicle. After washing her hands, she walked past the group of women again, and headed through the toilet door, back into the club. The kick from the bass reverberated in her chest; she was no longer simply listening to the music, she was feeling it.

She slithered past a few people who were dancing outside the toilets, and walked slowly into the direction of the dance floor, taking another drink from her bottle. Whilst descending the stairs, her shoulder caught the arm of another person dancing, and accidentally knocked them off balance. Before she could apologise, the newcomer turned around and stared at her. The immediate attraction from both parties was intense – the most captivating pair of green eyes stared right back at her, the best she'd ever seen. Without saying a word, she put her arms around the stranger's neck seductively, their eyes locked, they both opened their mouths and they kissed.

May 2013

Deborah Lewis

Deborah looked at the black leather gimp mask. The soft black leather surface, the zipped up mouth, the dull shine under the lights. The feature-less dead holes posing as eyes stared back at her.

Why would anyone want, no, need something as ugly as this to assist with their sex life.

She considered it an awful looking garment. Day in, day out, she had the displeasure of ogling it from the counter of the shop where she worked. On several occasions, she'd asked her boss to remove it, or put it on display in another part of the store, but he insisted that it stay in its home near the tills as a centre display, an impulse purchase, for the more adventurous customer.

Horrible thing.

It wasn't all that bad working in a sex shop. Deborah already had twelve months under her belt. Sure, she got some funky customers now and again, and the odd pervert, but the pay was surprisingly good, the hours were flexible, and the best part were the free toys that she could take home to add harmonious variety to her own sex life.

Deborah wasn't really much to look at. Her curly black hair was usually greasy and tied back in a loose ponytail. She had a pale, pasty face with sunken eyes that she usually coated with too much garish make-up. Her choice in clothes was usually something seedy or dark; gothic, one of the few things her boss liked about her. He thought her image was a good representation of the theme of the store. She was still unsure as to whether this was a good thing.

The shop was small and over stocked, tucked

away in a back street in the Cheetham Hill district of Manchester – an area infamous for its open prostitution and red light activity. Every evening, working girls lived up to their reputation on the streets. It was also a haven for potent gun crime and heavy drug use. The shop had blacked out windows, for privacy and security. A simple banner spooled across the front window saying, *Private Shop*.

Most of the people that visited the store were strangers. There were only a few people that she could ever recall seeing more than once. Customers would vary from young men, looking sheepishly for the latest film or magazine release, to couples looking for ways to liven up their sex lives. It was a rare occasion when she would meet someone interested in the real kinky stuff – like the gimp mask.

Today, trade in the shop had been particularly slow. There had been one middle-aged man, earlier that afternoon, just after she had started her shift. He had purchased some skimpy underwear for his wife, claiming that it was their wedding anniversary. With a sly wink, he joked that the gift was really for him. It had made her skin crawl.

Another young man entered about thirty minutes ago, looking nervous and uncomfortable. He had loitered around the video section for about twenty minutes before choosing a couple of titles. Deborah loved the nervous ones. She did her best to give him her patented *you filthy pervert* look as he paid. She noticed that he was actually shaking as he fumbled to get his credit card into the pin machine. Sometimes it was fun.

Taking the opportunity for a quick toilet break while the shop was so quiet, she quickly walked through the door behind the counter. She wasn't surprised that, on her return, the shop remained empty. She looked at the time on her phone.

15:15 – only another five hours to go.

She yawned.

If it remained this quiet, she would consider closing early.

She checked her phone for text messages or missed phone calls; there were none. She quickly tapped on the app that opened up her Facebook profile. A quick scan of her page revealed that there wasn't much going on in the outside world – even her social media life was having a slow day. Suddenly, the bell chimed on the door, making her jump as a customer entered the shop.

Looking up from her phone, she watched someone enter the shop, nodding slightly in acknowledgement as the customer walked over to the magazine section, and started to browse quietly. Returning her attention to her phone, she loaded up her Twitter account, desperate to find something that may spark up a bit of interest on such a dull afternoon.

Whilst reading a particularly dull tweet from a so-called celebrity, one detailing her latest purchase of ugly clothing, a metallic clunking sound on the counter made her jump. Looking up from her phone, the customer stood before her smiling. Deborah was completely taken aback; she could sense the oozing sex appeal and sheer confidence emanating from the stranger. Staring back at her was the most captivating pair of green eyes that she had ever seen.

Fumbling clumsily, she put her phone down behind the till and apologised. She looked down to the counter at the purchases before scanning the barcodes on the items; two pairs of solid steel handcuffs.

Killer's Got A Gunn

Julie Shields

The excitement runs rapidly through every fibre of my body. I can barely contain it. I feel like a child on Christmas Eve, this is the best part. The build-up. The anticipation.

It all comes down to this.

I inspect the deserted building from where I stand – an old industrial unit in Salford, which originally manufactured steel tube products. Once a hive of productivity, it is now reduced to a crumbling wreck, a mere shadow of its former self.

Overhead, various skylights have been smashed by the irresponsible teenagers who clambered onto the roof for reckless perusal of stimulation in their otherwise dull lives, leaving filthy shards of jagged glass littering the factory's concrete floor. The corner of a steel shutter beneath a goods inwards sign remains buckled at one end of the factory, allowing access to the building.

I've been frequenting these premises on every single night for the past two weeks, ensuring that the place is secure and void of any unwanted attention. In that time, I've not received a single, unwelcome visitor. The last thing I need is a tramp or security guard turning up unannounced, and interrupting me while I work.

A fifteen tonne goods crane casts a dominant shadow from above; it runs the entire length of the factory, down a solid steel track. Hanging down from the gantry, a solid, steel chain drapes over a cast iron hook. She is suspended from the hook by her wrists - attached by two pairs of steel handcuffs that cut deep into the soft flesh, her ankles bound by thick black duct tape.

I watch her sleep; she looks peaceful. Her ragged mop of brown hair mats to her head with sweat and dirt. She has a small, beautiful mouth with thin lips, and delicate facial features.

She does have a lovely smile.

A small silver piercing protrudes from her right eyebrow. She dangles naked, like a slab of meat, her clothes ripped off and thrown in a pile on the floor beside her. Her taste in clothes is impeccable, if you disregard the ridiculously thick, multi coloured headband that I ripped off earlier.

Her body is perfect: large, round breasts, smooth olive skin. Her slim stomach widens out in the right places into childbearing hips. Unfortunately, children is something she will never have.

Its time.

"Wake up."

No response.

"Wake up." I say it again, louder.

Nothing. No response whatsoever.

I slap her sharply around the cheek. Still she sleeps; she could be bluffing. Annoyed, I grab her chin firmly between my thumb and fingers and raise her face towards me. I bite down into her piercing and through her eyebrow. The crunching sensation feels similar to eating sushi - I bite through with my front teeth and tear away the flesh. The texture of steel and the taste of warm, coppery liquid fills my mouth. She wakes up in surprise, screaming in agony and biting down into the rubber ball gag – I spit the piercing and a mouthful of blood into her face. She winces and attempts to pull away as the blood and saliva slither down her visage. It runs down her brow and into her eyes.

Continuing to grunt and beginning to hyperventilate, her eyes dart around to inspect her current location. She recognises me, I can tell. The look of confusion and fear on her face is truly remarkable. I embrace the feeling of pure empowerment.

A steady dribble of blood runs from the jagged opening above her eye, down her face, and begins to trickle over her right breast. I caress the blood around the nipple slowly feeling it begin to stiffen at my touch. She moans slightly from beneath the ball gag.

"You like that, don't you? You filthy slut!"

She purrs and nods. Unfortunately for her, this is a tactic that I am well aware of; attempting to gain a level of trust in the hope that I may be convinced to release her – pathetic. For now, I will play along. I lean forward and whisper softly, directly into her ear.

"Will you pleasure me if I agree to let you go?"

Frantically nodding her head, she begins grunting from behind the gag. I move my hand down between her legs and begin to caress the opening of her vagina with my index finger. She moans slightly as I insert my middle finger and slowly draw it backwards and forwards, feeling her natural lubricant beginning to flow.

She closes her eyes and begins to moan with pleasure. Withdrawing my hand, I take a step back and bend down, collecting one of the filthy shards of broken glass from the factory floor.

"Well, now that you're greased up and ready to go."

Her eyes snap open wide in terror. She begins frantically shaking her head. I hear muffled screams from behind the gag. I hold up the shard in front of her face; it's about the length of a paring knife. Her eyes gaze at the glass and she begins to convulse. I gently ran my thumb over the razor sharp tip. The tip catches a reflection from the strip lights above and shines into her eye.

I laugh. "You may want to see about getting a tetanus shot."

Even muffled by the gag, her scream is almost

deafening as I thrust the makeshift weapon between her legs, tearing and dragging backwards and forwards. A sickening ripping sound echoes around the warehouse as a torrent of liquid and gore splashes to the floor in a pool below her.

Her legs buckle, unable to sustain her body weight any longer. She drops, suspended only by her wrists. I can see the damage that the cuffs are doing to the flesh as she hangs. Her violent sobbing continues, and her breathing becomes deeper, more laboured.

I grab her chin and raise her face level with mine, eye to eye. Her face is completely pale, her eyes sunk into large, black rings. The texture of her skin and lips is mottled. A thick stream of sweat runs from her forehead, and down her cheeks. Her eyes stare back at mine – afraid, hurt, and defeated.

I wink. "Don't you get going to sleep on me yet, woman."

Turning and reaching into my kit bag, I remove my first item – a costotome; a surgical device used during post mortem examinations for cutting through ribs. In her current position, hanging from the crane and suspended by her arms, both sides of her rib cage are perfectly exposed. I thrust the tool forward and upwards just below her bottom left rib. Her head lurches back in pain as the metal punctures the skin with a sickening squelching sound. Her muffled screaming continues, blood spraying off her lips. The volume and intensity increases as I cut through the first rib with the device – it gives off a satisfying, cracking sound as the bone snaps.

I repeat the action, this time below her right rib. Again, I hear the splendid cracking sound from the breaking of bone; her muffled cries of agony continue.

I throw the tool back into my kit bag and inspect my work so far. She's lost a lot of blood, and is in a weakened state. Her body is drenched in sweat and crimson. I doubt that she will last much longer.

I approach her. She barely has the strength to lift her head to look at me. Her eyes are beginning to roll back into her skull. She mumbles something from behind the ball gag. Unable to make out what she is saying, I unfasten the buckles that hold it in place. It drops to the floor.

Barely audible, she asks, "Why?"

I laughed. "Why? Because I can. Because I want to. You're an unfortunate pawn in a much larger game. There are always plenty of sluts like you out there who are willing to jump into bed with a complete stranger."

She raised her head slightly. "Just kill me."

I sneer. "Oh I intend to, princess, don't you worry about that."

Returning to my kit bag, I pull out another item – a cordless angle grinder. I snap the battery to ensure that it's in place, before clicking the power button. The circular disc quickly spins to life, as do the orbs in the head of my victim. The noise of the power tool makes her stare intently with dread.

"Do you remember earlier in the evening when I said you have a lovely smile?" I ask, looking at the tool. "Well I meant it, but there is always room for improvement."

I press the power button once more and lock it into position forcing the disc to gyrate violently. I slowly approach, her eyes fixated in abject terror at the circular grinding disc, rotating quickly and slowly as I inch it towards her face. With a fluid movement, I grab a handful of her sweaty hair in my left hand and thrust forward with the power tool in my right, straight into the opening of her screaming mouth.

The disc cuts through the flesh like a hot knife through butter, until it hits her back teeth. I continue pushing and yanking the tool up and down, spraying myself with her warm blood and fleshy gore. Teeth fragments began to chip and snap away and fly off in every direction, like shrapnel from a grenade.

Keeping a grip on her blood and sweat soaked scalp, I continue to hold her head in place for a few more seconds and continue with the grinder. Her eyes begin to roll back in her head and she gives off a sickening, wet, gargling sound. I release the power button on the hand tool and pull it away, the disc dripping with blood, lumps of wet flesh, and enamel.

Her mouth drops open even further into an unnatural position; the inside of her mouth is a complete wreckage of broken teeth and torn, bloody flesh. Letting go of her hair, her head drops down to her chest with a wet thump.

Dead.

BOUND

By
Matt Hickman
&
Andrew Lennon

DCI Mark Gunn

Homicide

His bitter odour entered the room before he did. A mixture of last night's coffee and the two routine morning cigarettes. He stood at a dominant six foot six, with thinning blond hair and a naturally large frame, which, during his later years, had started to expand excessively larger around his mid-section. The dark rings around his eyes spoke of a workaholic, a man married to this vocation.

DCI Mark Gunn placed his empty mug on the kitchen counter and filled it with warm coffee from the jug. He hated that mug. On the side, it said *World's Best Policeman*, a blatant lie, if there ever was one. Gunn wasn't even the stations best police officer, but he was consistent. He got results and he got them more often, and quickly, than most of his colleagues.

Growing up in a council estate in Cardiff, Gunn learnt how to fight from a very young age. At the age of ten, he was already as tall as most teenagers. This made him a regular target for the most ambitious of bullies. He looked clumsy and slow, because he was so much bigger than most of his friends. On one occasion, as a group of teens were passing, they automatically assumed that he was some kind of weirdo, someone that didn't have any friends of his own age. When he revealed his age, this brought on even more ridicule.

People called him names like freak, Bigfoot, and string bean. All of the other kids his age got away unscathed, but Gunn was subject to the constant shouts and teasing, every time they crossed paths.

What started as simple name callIng quickly escalated when Gunn dared to mutter the words, "fuck off," in response to one of the teens, who had just called him a lanky streak of piss. The teenager, Paul Jones, was of average size for a fourteen-year-old, but that still made him a fair bit smaller than Gunn. Even so, he wasn't going to have some kid telling him to fuck off. Jones didn't even shout anything in response; he just ran straight at Gunn and punched him in the face. Gunn fell backwards onto the ground. His eyes filled with tears, not from pain or emotion, but because the punch had caught him on the nose, and simply made his eyes water.

Before Gunn had the chance to realise what was going on, he heard loud chants start to rise from the surrounding children.

"*Fight, fight, fight, fight.*"

Wiping the tears from his eyes, Gunn looked up to see Jones standing in what looked like a classic boxing stance. This was going to be his very first fight. He could barely stand himself up; he was shaking with primitive fear. He lifted his hands up before him; he felt that was the right thing to do.

Over his balled fists, Gunn could see the snarling face of Jones staring back at him. Jones threw a right, smacking Gunn viciously on the cheek. He threw another right, then another, and another. Gunn's head didn't really move from the impact of the punches. He didn't notice at the time, but afterwards he came to realise that the punches hadn't really hurt that much either.

A random onlooker shouted, "Don't just stand there, punch him back!"

Gunn took another punch to the face; he balled his fist tight until his hand was shaking uncontrollably. He let out a loud, animalistic roar and swung his arm down, and then back up into a powerful uppercut that caught Jones right on the chin. The older boy lifted an inch before dropping like a heavy sack to the ground.

Gunn could still remember the look on the faces

of the audience when they heard that boy's jaw breaking, their utter silence. He could also remember the feeling he had when he looked down at his fallen body. Something inside him had been unleashed; it was something violent and brutal.

And he liked it.

In his late teens, Gunn put his skills to good use. He was part of a 'firm', a loose term coined by the press, and their bitter enemies. The public referred to them as football hooligans. It wasn't quite the mindless violence that Gunn had grown accustomed to. Fights were organised by the top boys in the group, usually scheduled to coincide with a meet up with their team's opponents the following week.

Cardiff's 'firm' was not great, they mostly had a lot of wasters, guys that would talk the talk, but when it came to the fight, they became mere spectators. Cardiff did have a select few who could *really* fight, the men that lived for it, breathed it. Given the opportunity, they would do it as a day job. Eight hours a day, six days a week.

Gunn was one of those guys.

Usually while the rest of the firm were getting knocked to the ground or running away, Gunn was taking on three or four at a time. The more he took a hit, the more he seemed to enjoy it, as if the pain gave him more strength. For a brief period, he inherited the nickname 'Hulk'. That didn't last; the decision in the pub was unanimous; the nickname 'Gunn' had more impact.

In 1993, Cardiff Football Club had cemented their promotion out of Division Three. A huge travelling crowd arrived at Scunthorpe, all wearing fancy dress. Many of the men dressed as women. When the final whistle blew and Cardiff won by three goals to zero, the fans took to the pitch.

Announcements came over the tannoy.

"Please stay off the pitch, fans, please stay off

the pitch."

The fans ignored the requests and began singing.

"*We are the championsssss.*"

Hundreds of men, all dressed as women, stormed the pitch. This momentous event earned the title of the '1993 tranny pitch invasion.' Gunn was amongst the so-called trannies. At his size and stature, being dressed as a woman was a monstrosity in itself. He frightened children as he walked past with his blonde wig, muscular hairy legs, and his big Neanderthal grin.

Post-game rituals occurred as normal. The firm found the nearest pub and proceeded to drink as much as they could. With the majority of them being close to or over six foot, and wearing bright floral dresses; they didn't exactly blend into the crowd. It wasn't long before a gang of Scunthorpe fans entered the pub. They were quick to shout abuse. Gunn immediately wanted to retaliate, but his company had told him to relax. It was all in good fun, everyone was in a good mood after the victory.

"I tell you what," a Scunthorpe fan pointed to Gunn. "That big bitch one can get down on her knees and suck my cock."

Before anyone had chance to stop him, Gunn shoved his pint glass into the fans face. The glass didn't shatter like it does in the movies, it broke into several large pieces, one of which went straight through his eye. The screams made everyone stop in their tracks. For a moment, beside the wails and shouts of pain, the pub fell into silence. Following that was nothing short of chaos. The fight spilled out from the pub and onto the streets. Hundreds of football fans threw punches and kicks. The violence was catastrophic, and it wasn't long until bottles and bricks were thrown into the mix.

Gunn noticed one fan running away, down a side

alley. He was quick to pursue him; he eventually caught the man from behind and rammed his face into a wall. As the blood ran from the man's nose, a police officer walked past the alley. He stopped for a moment and glanced towards Gunn and his victim, curious.

The fan begged for help in the only way he knew. "Oi, you fucking cunt! Don't just watch, come and help me!"

Gunn had slowly started to creep from the alley, in the opposite direction.

"Now, hang on a minute. Who do you think you're talking to?" The officer replied.

"You, you bastard! Come and…"

Before he could finish, the officer drove a knee straight into his stomach.

"Call me a bastard, will ya?"

He grabbed him by the neck and started to drag him out of the alley.

"Oi lads, I've got one here for ya."

As a police van was pulling alongside him, the fan started to fight back. He threw one wild punch and caught the policeman on the side of the head. Before he had chance to throw another, he had five policemen on top of him, three restraining him, while the other two delivered hard punches to the side of his head. The assaulted officer walked alongside, holding his nose. He took a run up and kicked the fan in the stomach, hard and brutal, as if he was taking a penalty kick in the Cup Final.

Gunn watched in awe from the alley. He saw how the officers completely manhandled the fan, how they all worked as a cohesive unit, got the job done, and then threw him in the back of the van. The fan would be arrested, there was no doubt, but nothing would happen to the men who assaulted him. Right there and then, Gunn decided he wanted to be part of a team like that. The owner of a licence to do damage with no questions asked.

The ultimate firm.

It didn't take long for Gunn to learn that life on the police force wasn't quite the free pass he'd dreamed of, but it turned out he was good at it. He naturally had the mind of a criminal, he knew how they thought and therefore he knew how and where to catch them. If he needed a bit of information every now and then, he didn't mind bending the rules and using his muscle, and natural talent to get what he needed.

Some people didn't like the way he worked, but what mattered were results. Gunn got the job done and in doing so, he earned himself a reputation as one of the best on the force. He worked his way up until finally his results earned him the dream position: a Detective Chief Inspector in homicide. With this new spate of murders, Gunn had authorisation to put his own team together. His squad of four would form the murder investigation team that was going to crack this case. He was sure of it, and if not, he was at least willing to put his life on the line trying.

Melissa Lason

A tiny dark haired girl pulled at the bottom of her mother's dress.

"Mama," Melissa called.

"Not now, darling. Go and play."

The tiny child toddled off to play with her puzzle box. She picked up a square shaped block and placed it in the square hole, and then picked up the triangle block and placed that one in the triangular hole. At eighteen months old, Melissa had already learned to entertain herself. She had taken a liking to puzzle toys. Anything that required a good amount of thought and element of problem solving seemed to grasp her attention.

Growing up in Arizona, with a negligent mother who never changed her ways because she was never caught, Melissa learned to adapt quickly. The desert-like environment had the potential to kill off any unattended, unmonitored child. She had quickly learned that she needed to be inside during the mid-afternoon hours, and she ensured that she drank enough water, drinking straight from the outside tap.

Of course, she couldn't do any of this until she was around fifteen months old. Her mother supplied food and drink as required, but it had been to the bare minimum. As a baby, she cried too much according to her mother. Even then, she craved too much attention. Her mother was delighted when Melissa was able to fend for herself. This meant one less job as a disinterested mother. She kept some milk near the bottom of the fridge so Melissa could help herself. The only thing she had to do was cook her meals, which was easy seeing as she made just a little more of her own meal, enough for a kid's side portion.

Melissa couldn't wait until she turned five; she

was able to start school. She had seen it on television and fell in love at the sight of it. A place where she would be assigned tasks that would stimulate her mind, and given puzzles to solve. She could even make some friends. Her mother was equally excited because it meant that Melissa would now be out of her hair, for at least a couple of hours every day. She walked Melissa to school for her first day, but gave Melissa strict instructions to pay attention to the route, because she wouldn't be collecting her for the return trip.

Melissa's keen eye made it easy for her to remember the route, to and from school. The schoolwork proved to be easy for her as well. In fact, it was a lot easier than she had anticipated; it didn't prove to be much of a challenge. She flew through the daily tasks until the teacher had nothing left to give her. After, the teacher told her to sit and read until the day was over. This alienated her from the other children. They didn't like the girl that finished all of the day's work with hours to go, while they were still struggling to grasp it. It made them feel stupid. As a result, Melissa's dream circle of friends never existed, and she didn't have a group to socialise with.

Melissa loved the walk to and from school. She had to pass Salt River, a beautiful spot of paradise that seemed misplaced in this desert land. Sometimes she would see wild horses drinking from the river. It was in these moments, stood watching the majestic creatures, that she was happiest. Sometimes she dreamed of being one of these horses, having the ability to run like the wind and escape to somewhere else.

Anywhere else.

In October of 1983, Melissa got her wish. The remnants of a tropical storm brought so much rain to Phoenix that the Gila River overflowed, breaking its banks. Fourteen people died due to the flooding.

Melissa and her mother survived, but their house did not, destroyed along with more than eight hundred other homes, which totalled about five hundred million dollars in damage.

Melissa's mother had insurance on her home. Despite her shortcomings, she saw fit to cover the house for natural disaster damage. The flood had scared her so much that she chose to leave Phoenix, instead of paying to have a new home built. After a quick survey on the current state of her life, she decided that she didn't just want to get out of Phoenix. She wanted to leave America completely.

She packed their bags and they moved to England, Manchester to be more specific. Things didn't change much at home for Melissa. Her mother still ignored her, only now she ignored her to spend time with a different circle of friends. Melissa, however, was still a loner. Initially her classmates thought it was cool to share the class with an American, but very shortly after, they realised that Melissa was too intelligent for them to interact with, and Melissa realised that she just didn't care for friends anymore. So, she focused all of her attention on puzzles and problem solving games.

Melissa's teen years in high school and college were identical to her younger years. She spent most of her time alone and she spent all of that time with her head buried in puzzles. As soon as she turned eighteen, she signed up to join the police. After watching countless movies and television shows, she decided that being part of the police force would be an excellent use of her skills. She knew that she could have solved every problem on those shows. Yes, of course, real life would be different, but she had to try.

She was born to do it.

Melissa had to pass a tough ritual of training, which she did easily. Her fitness level was surprisingly excellent, considering she didn't actively partake in sports, but she always restricted her diet, ensuring she never touched any of the unhealthy food her mother offered.

It didn't take long; after being in the force for a few months, her keen eye became an asset. Various visits to random houses that Melissa had attended, sometimes just for observation and training, led to arrests based on clues that Melissa noticed on the premises. She had never been in any position where she had to analyse the crime scene for a murder, until now. When DCI Gunn informed her that she was now part of his team, she felt ecstatic. Gunn had always worked homicide, and this was her time to shine. Her whole life had been building up to this point.

Charlie Corkish

Fingers moved like lightning, typing various codes and passwords, and other significant numbers that the rest of the team didn't understand. Charlie was working on cracking one of the blood-soaked laptops discovered at the crime scene.

"I'm in!" Charlie threw her hands up in the air in celebration.

"Right," said Gunn. "Let's see what type of conversations this girl has been having."

"No problem." Charlie's lightning fingers went to work again.

Charlie grew in up a small Irish town named Wicklow. Her group of friends were small, but they were very close. They would always look out for each other. Sometimes they felt like they lived in the middle of nowhere, like the world was moving on, passing all of them by as they simply existed in their seaside town.

As with most small towns, there never really seemed to be much happening. They had to make their own entertainment. Charlie had fond memories of going to the Black Castle, the ruins on an old Norse castle located in Wicklow. It sat on a cliff on the sea front, which supposedly had caves used by smugglers once upon a time, but Charlie and her friends never found them. Once, Charlie, being the crazy one in her group, dived off the cliffs to see if she could get a better look. Completely misjudging the current, she didn't actually get to see anything. Instead, she almost drowned in the sea, saved by the coastguard a few hours later. It was quite a big story at the time, but one that Charlie soon forgot.

It took a couple of days in bed, but Charlie recovered. Luckily, with no injuries or long-term sickness, it didn't take much time for her to get back out with the gang. She went to the woods, a place they called 'Parkers'.

Charlie beckoned to her friends. "Hey!"

"Oh, look who's back!" Brian laughed. "It's Ireland's most famous cliff diver."

"Fuck you," Charlie said, but she followed with a wry smile, to show that she was just playing.

"Come on then, big shot. Let's see how you do on this now."

Brian stood up on a hill, holding a rope swing, which hung from the highest branch on a grand oak tree. The swing went over the widest patch of a river and led to a platform on the other side. The kids always challenged each other to see who could actually make it across to the platform. If they couldn't then they would end up in the river, and pulling themselves out soaking wet. It took them a while but most of the kids got used to it. After much practice, they were getting to the platform almost every time. Except Charlie. She could never time the jump right, and because of that, she spent most of her time in the river.

"Oh, come on, Brian. You know I can't do that."

"Give it a try. You never know. After your deep-sea dive, you might have found some secret power. Or at least a sense of timing," Brian laughed.

Charlie sighed and made her way up the hill. She knew how it worked. After being challenged, she couldn't say no. When she reached Brian, he handed her the rope. His face wore a large grin, a smug smile that Charlie wanted to punch, but she restrained herself. She was going to do it this time.

She would wipe that smile off his face by landing on the platform.

She grabbed the rope and walked a little further up the hill. Staring at the platform on the other side, it seemed so far away. She'd done this jump a hundred times before, but it was further than she remembered.

Right, come on, Charlie. You can do this.

She jumped off and pulled herself up onto the rope, wrapping her legs around so her backside sat on a large knot tied into it. The wind blew in her face. She let out a loud yell as her hair flew behind her.

"Whooo!"

Glancing down, she could see the drop to the river and the thought entered her mind; that water is going to be ice cold.

It's October for God's sake. Charlie, you idiot, it's going to be freezing.

But it doesn't matter this time, because you're going to land on the platform.

Before she had time to continue this argument with herself, the platform was beneath her. She unhooked her legs from the rope and threw herself through the air. The wooden ledge seemed to grow as she was getting closer to it.

She was going to make it.

She could turn round and laugh in Brian's face.

She was going to do it.

Her feet landed on the wood, making a thudding sound at she hit it. Charlie threw her arms up in the air. Not in celebration, but in an attempt to try and keep her balance. She landed right on the edge, teetering on his toes. As she straightened, she stood upright, and her body began to lean backwards over the edge.

Almost like a cartoon, she swung her arms around in circles trying to regain her balance. She could hear Brian laughing at her from the other side of the river.

"Arsehole!"

It was the only thing she managed to say before she tumbled backwards, and descended to the ice cold river below.

After a moment, Charlie's head came out of the

water. Brian, along with a couple of her other friends, were pointing and laughing. Charlie had to accept it; it must have looked hilarious. She did the only thing she could do and laughed along with them.

Charlie first got her taste of computers in the local video arcade, Tony's. She developed a bit of an addiction to the game, Haley's Comet, but it wasn't long before that addiction turned into something else. She wanted to do more than just play on computers. She wanted to know what was in them, and how they worked. What magical things did the plastic box hold that created all of these wonderful games and pictures on the screen?

After a long wait, and months of begging to her parents repeatedly, Charlie got her chance to see how it all worked. At that time, computers were very expensive, her parents couldn't afford to buy her one and she knew that, so she didn't ask. What she did ask for was the opportunity to work in the field, to go on a computer-training course at the local college. It was a weekend course and meant for adults, but Charlie was a bright kid, and she knew she would be able to keep up.

Computers were the future. Everyone who had any common sense knew that. They knew that, eventually, everyone would be working on one or with a computer in one way or another. Charlie wanted more than that; she didn't just want to work *on* a computer, she wanted to have her mind inside it.

The training course was like Pandora's Box for Charlie. It opened a whole world of magical creation and technological wonders. Most of the other people on the course, adults in particular, said that it was like rocket science, and that no one other than a genius could understand that.

However, Charlie did.

She took in everything that the tutor taught. She

took heavy notes, and later on, she paid a visit to the local library and signed out some books, to build on the basic knowledge she had gained.

When she finished with school, Charlie went to college and studied I.T., along with a couple of other subjects. She carried her journey of education on to university. She moved from her little town of Wicklow in Ireland and took up her studies in Manchester. To begin with, she lived on campus, but shortly after she found a flat, one she could rent for herself. It was perfect for her needs. A simple one bedroom abode, a kitchen, bathroom and a living room, the latter of which was kitted out from wall to wall with high tech computers, hooked up to multiple screens.

Charlie breezed through her studies and graduated from Manchester with a master's degree in computer science. As fate would have it, a week after she graduated, she was contacted by the local police force. They were recruiting, more specifically, they were looking for someone who could work with I.T. A contact at the university told them that Charlie was one of the best they would find.

They invited her to an interview. She was given a computer, along with a handful of tasks that she had to prove she was capable of passing. Within an hour of completing those tests, she was informed that she wouldn't be suitable for the job that was advertised, which was to develop a very basic software program for the Manchester Metropolitan Police force's computer system.

Instead, they offered her a job working with various units within the force. Whether it be the drug squad, or the murder investigation team. They wanted her as their personal on-call hacker. This was the dream job for Charlie, the sort of thing she lived for. She always thought that nothing could beat the thrill of hacking into someone's computer system, but now she was going to find out how much of a thrill it was to hack into a system, and crack a murder case.

Charlie's record was flawless. She could get into any computer. Now, she found herself assigned to the murder investigation team, to help investigate the murder of three local girls. The large detective shoved a laptop into her hands.

"Get into that," he said, with no smile.

Charlie looked into the man's eyes. She could see years of pent-up stress in those orbs, a story she would love to hear one day. She glanced over his shoulder. Sat in the office behind him were two other women, one blonde, and one with black hair. The blonde looked very nervous, like she didn't know what she was doing there. Unlike the dark one, who looked to have the same vibe as Charlie. Confidence oozed from her.

She felt a little push and looked back up to the DCI again.

"Please," his smiled widened.

"On it."

Jessica Sinnamond

Biting her finger nails down as far as she could without drawing blood, Jessica glanced over to the woman who had entered the room. The woman had only just walked in, and the DCI shoved a laptop into her hands. DCI Gunn seemed to be a bit of a hard case. Jessica felt as though her stomach was in knots. She couldn't believe that she had landed on this team, both thrilled and terrified at the same time. The one thing that helped her nerves was Melissa. She was also from America, granted she was from Arizona rather than Pennsylvania, but still, it felt like a little piece of home was there with her. Lately, that memory of home seemed to be further away than ever.

Jessica was a popular girl when growing up, she was always surrounded by her friends. She was in *that* crowd; every school has a crowd like it. The group that every kid wants to be a part of. The girls were beautiful, all cheerleaders, their boyfriends all ripped to the bone at a young age, all jocks, of course.

If you asked her about her life, Jessica would give one answer: Perfect. She had no idea where she was going, or what she was going to do after school. She didn't think any further than that exact moment, because the moment was perfect, and why would you want to miss that thinking about anything else?

After a great party, Jessica's friend, Matt, drove her home. She always loved Matt's company; as a cheerleader, people considered it 'cool' to have a token gay best friend, and Matt was it. He never failed to make her laugh. She gave him a kiss on the cheek and then jumped out of his car. As always, he dropped her off at the end of her road. He sat in the car and watched as she walked to her house.

Jessica hugged herself, rubbing her arms to keep warm as she followed the tracks along the stream. She stopped for a moment when she thought she heard a noise. She looked into the large field opposite, the stream trickling in the quiet air. The darkness stared back at her, leaving her with nothing to see.

"*Faggot!*" someone called from behind her.
BANG!

Jessica dropped to the floor at the sound of gunfire; she held her hands over her head and closed her eyes. Panic started to take over, she struggled to breathe, the realisation of what she had just heard overcame her. Tears began rolling down her cheeks; they began to pool in the dirt beneath her. It felt like a lifetime, but only a few seconds had passed by the time she stood back up. She knew exactly where the shot had come from.

"*Matt!*" she screamed.

Sprinting towards the car, her vision blurred, she could hear her father calling from behind. When she got there, Matt was staring into her eyes. He slumped half hanging out of the car, his head upside down, his dead stare unmoving. Jessica held him in her arms as she cried and screamed for help. She looked around for signs of the gunman, but whoever it was, was long gone, the darkness aiding them in their getaway.

Matt's killer was never found.

The police deemed the crime a hate attack. The police made a thorough investigation, but as Jessica was the only witness, and she had nothing to offer other than the sound of gunfire, no evidence was left behind. After a while, the case just sort of whittled off and died.

After Matt's death, something was born inside Jessica. She developed a hunger to prevent such crimes from happening in the future. She stopped living in her dreamland of cheerleaders and jocks and parties, and she started to focus of what she needed to do to gain a career in law enforcement. She trained every day, and she studied as much as she could. It became an obsession; all that mattered now was that she became a cop.

After many arguments with her parents, circumstances where taken out of her hands. Her father had to move to England because of work. Jessica was only eighteen, and as much as she told her parents that she could leave and live by herself, she knew the truth. Even though she was old enough to live on her own, she couldn't financially survive on her own. Her dreams of making it into the police force would have been lost while working in a 7/11 every day, to make enough money to make the rent.

Instead, she latched on to the next best thing.

Her father researched various universities in England. She told him no. The only way that she would go with them is if she could sign up to the police force in England. After looking into it a bit more, they realised that she needed to be a resident in the country for more than three years before she could apply. So, for those three years, she would continue her training and studying to help her get in when it came to her application. Three months after joining the force, she rented a place and moved in with her partner, Alex, a medical supplies driver that worked in and around the city.

Of course, after all her years of preparation, Jessica walked into the police force with no problems at all. As with any job, she started from the bottom, and she was fine with that, walking the beat along with her colleagues.

They received a call reporting complaints for loud music. The house in question was on the street next to them, so they called in that they were already there and made their way to the house.

When they knocked on the door, there was no response. The music was loud and probably the reason for their knock going unheard. Again, she knocked on the door, this time it was more of a hammering. A man opened it, his face drawn and thin, his hair long and greasy, hanging across his face. Jessica's colleague asked him to turn the music down and let them in. The man obliged.

Inside, he sat on an old stained sofa, biting at his nails. His hands were shaking rapidly; the tell-tale signs of a drug addict in desperate need of a fix. The placed smelled foul, as was usually the case in drug dens. Jessica could see that nothing they were saying to the man was registering. He just kept biting his nails and glancing towards the door on the other side of the room. Something in Jessica's stomach tightened, she couldn't explain what it was, but she knew that something wasn't right. As if he could read her mind, the man's glances to the closed room became even more rapid. Jessica stood up and walked to the door.

"Um, errrr … what are you doing?" the man asked.

Jessica didn't respond. She continued toward the door.

"Hey, you can't just go in there. No stop…"

Jessica opened the door.

The smell almost made her throw up. Her mind flashed back to that time so many years ago, and now she stood there once again, with dead eyes staring into hers. The bottom half of the face was missing, as though some wild beast had ripped the jaw from it. She had no idea how long the body had been lying in that bathtub, but it certainly wasn't a recent death.

She heard the man behind her bolt from the couch and run towards the front door of the house.

Glancing at her colleague to see that he remained still, jaw dropped and doing nothing at all, she chose to give chase herself.

All of the training paid off. The man didn't even get a hundred metres from the house before Jessica was upon him. She tackled him to the ground and easily slipped him into handcuffs. Several minutes after she called it in, her colleague showed his face again from the house. Shortly after that, a whole team arrived and took it out of Jessica's hands.

It turned out that the body in the bathtub was the drug addict's girlfriend. He told his interviewer that she had tried to steal his fix so he hit her over the head with an ashtray. When she saw the blood pouring from her head, she screamed. It was so loud that he was scared it would attract attention from the neighbours. He stamped on her mouth to shut her up, and then he stamped again, and again, until even the gurgling sound had stopped. After that, he said no amount of drugs would remove the sounds of those screams from his head. That's why he had the music so loud; to try and drown it out. It didn't work.

Jessica's actions had stirred up some chatter within the station. The rookie girl who found, solved and the caught the suspect of a murder, all on her own within a year of joining the force. She inherited names like 'Robogirl', and 'Maniac Cop'. She also earned the chance of a lifetime.

She caught the attention of DCI Gunn.

Within a couple of weeks, she was assigned to his team. The term 'being thrown in at the deep end' could not even begin to describe her situation. She knew what this team was. She was going to be assisting in the hunt of a major serial killer, one that was picking off young girls. This was everything she had been working toward and now it was finally here, and it terrified her.

16th July 2013

Greater Manchester Police Station

The circular fan spinning overhead did nothing to cool down the heated air in the station's meeting room. It was almost unbearable. Under DCI Mark Gunn's instructions, the team had set up their investigation headquarters in the largest meeting room available.

The team had spent the last three days collating and comparing information, gathering evidence, and following any outstanding leads. Breaks were minimal; they had been working pretty solidly - fifteen-hour days.

Melissa had been running backwards and forwards to the lab with the slightest pieces of evidence that had been foraged and gathered from the scenes of the murders. Charlie had been painstakingly accessing online banking and phone records for each of the victims, and following up on their personal lives through various platforms of social media. Jessica spent the majority of the three days speaking to the families of the victims, trying to obtain any vital information that they might be missing.

Gunn looked around the faces of the members of the team that he had personally assigned. They all looked anxious. The humidity and heat of the office, due to the lack of proper air conditioning, combined with the pressure of the case, was making him increasingly agitated.

Placing his left fist into his right hand, he cracked his knuckles. Swapping his hands over, he cracked the knuckles on his right hand, slightly alleviating the pressure.

"So who wants to go first?" he asked.

They all looked at each other tentatively. Nobody

in the team responded.

"Okay," he continued. "Let's start with the first victim, Lucy French. Tell me what you know."

Charlie was the first to speak. "I checked her bank accounts. She lived off her husband's income. Not to the extent of a footballer's wife, but she did okay from him. Both current accounts and saving accounts were fine. No mounting debts. No strange payments to anyone."

Gunn Looked at Jessica. "What about the husband?"

"Clean as a whistle," Jessica began. "Gary French, a fairly successful businessman. He sells commodity steel products, nothing fancy. When I spoke to him, he seemed genuine, and heart-broken. He advised us that as far as he knew, Lucy had no enemies. She only really had a few close friends, and none of those were in contact with her that often."

"Does the husband have any women on the side?" Gunn asked.

"Not that I could make out. As far as I could tell, they were just an average couple, with no kids to complicate things. He goes to work to earn the money, and she goes to the salon to spend it on treatments."

Gunn pursed his lips. "What about her? Did she have a man on the side that the husband didn't know about?"

"Not as far as I can gather. She was apparently a very quiet woman. She had a tendency to keep herself to herself, her emails and social media were all virtually non-existent. I spoke to her friends; her husband gladly volunteered their details and none of them knew a thing. They were as shocked as anyone about her disappearance."

Gunn Looked at Melissa. "What do you have?"

Melissa opened the first manila file from the pile in front of her; it contained several photographs and case notes. She handed Gunn two of the photographs from inside.

Mark, exasperated, blew the air from his cheeks and held the photographs at arm's length, his mind trying to comprehend the horrific images before him. The body of a naked woman, prone and twisted in long grass. Her body lay sideways, exposing a series of appalling wounds scattered all over her abdomen.

He shook his head. "Holy shit."

"Holy shit is correct," she replied. "She was found by a man walking his dog early one morning in Alexandra Park. Her body had been left amongst the shrubs at the north end of the park; there was barely even an attempt to hide it."

Gunn was about to speak when Jessica interrupted. "We aren't treating him as a suspect. The poor man was so traumatised by the discovery that we had to offer him counselling. He's clean."

Gunn nodded a confirmation.

Melissa continued. "The post mortem showed that the most likely cause of death was the incision made across her throat, but this sick bastard made sure that she suffered first. Our inspection showed that there were other injuries all over her body – sixty-seven in total, all over her face, torso and back - totally butchered, and her teeth were smashed in with a heavy object. Even her husband was unsure at first, when we asked him to identify her. Whoever did this was one sick sonofabitch."

"Any signs of sexual abuse?"

"Not that we could tell, sir."

Gunn inspected the depravity depicted in the various photographs in front of him. The images were nearly enough to turn his stomach. The poor woman's body was peppered with cuts, bruises and burn marks. It was utterly sickening. The body, carelessly thrown down into the foliage, looked tragic, her dark eyes staring lifelessly at the camera.

Gunn had seen some disturbing things over the years. His mind drifted back to a case four years ago, where a hit and run driver had mowed down a fifteen-year-old girl. He had been the first to respond, and was on the scene before the ambulance arrived. Her ruined body lay twisted in the road, both of her legs broken, sharp bone poking through abraded flesh. She could barely breathe through internal trauma and bleeding.

The young girl had died in his arms. He thought back to the driver, claiming that his car was stolen from his driveway. However, Marks investigation showed that the times did not tie up. The man had never reported the stolen car until after the incident. Gunn had gotten that feeling in his gut, the one that was rarely wrong. He had visited the suspect's home after his release from questioning; he then proceeded to beat a confession from the man. Albeit a non-conventional method of getting a result, the police had apprehended a child killer. In the eyes of the public, and the girl's family, justice had been done. Gunn became an anti-hero in the eyes of the media.

The chilling image of that young child dying paled in comparison to the images that faced him now. He snapped back from his daydream.

He flicked the photographs back in Melissa's direction. She scooped them up from the desk and returned them to their place within the folder.

"Victim number two?" he asked, looking at nobody in particular.

"Vicky Stuart," Jessica responded.

Shuffling the manila folders in her hands, Melissa grabbed the one that displayed the victim's name in black marker pen, and threw it over to their team leader. Grabbing the folder from the desktop, Gunn opened the cover and his mouth dropped open in shock.

"What in the name of *God?*"

The pictures showed the remains of the body of a woman, lying on a filthy bed. The top half of her body had exposed muscle and tendons held together with dried blood and lumps of congealed flesh.

"He skinned her…" Melissa couldn't finish the sentence.

Gunn looked at her. "He what?"

"He removed the majority of the skin from her face, arms and body. The post mortem, however, shows that this was not the cause of death. The cause of the death was an overdose on heroin. A toxicology report showed that she had enough drugs in her system to take down an elephant. A lethal cocktail of heroin, ecstasy and cocaine."

Gunn looked at her. "So, she was already dead when this was done to her?"

"Yes," Melissa replied. "We found a puncture mark on what was left of her right arm."

"Just one? Was she an addict?"

"I checked with her family and friends," Jessica replied. "As far as anyone knew, she had never taken any drugs. She was pretty much against them. In fact, as far as they were concerned, she was as good as the girl next door."

Gunn rubbed his chin. "Any jilted ex-boyfriends?"

"No, she'd been single for a while from what her friends confirmed - nothing even casual now. She lived alone in an apartment on the edge of the city centre. She worked as a beautician. Her colleagues confirmed the same as her friends. She was a very quiet, shy girl. She mainly kept herself to herself."

"Parents?" asked Mark.

"Her parents are divorced; they have been since she was six-years-old. Her father lives in France, and she was never in contact with him. Her mother lives in Leeds."

"Has she been informed?"

"Yes, I went to see her personally. She broke

down in front of me when I told her, if she has anything to do with it, she's a great actor."

Gunn turned to Charlie. "What did you find out?"

"Pretty much nothing," she replied. "She was your average twenty-six-year-old. She lived in a rented apartment, no arrears, seemingly no other debts. Her mobile phone records indicate that she only spoke to a few real friends. Jessica has already been and spoken to them."

"What about her bank records? Were there any large cash withdrawals recently? Anything that could have indicated that she may have been in trouble?"

"No, nothing. Certainly nothing that would suggest that she was supporting a drug addiction."

Gunn looked at the mutilated remains of the girl on the picture in front of him, failing to piece anything together in his mind. Suddenly, he spotted the filthy bed sheets.

"Melissa, where was she found? Surely this wasn't her home?"

"No, she was found by a shop owner in an unused flat above a derelict shop on Moss Side. The property owner was informed when one of the other shop residents noticed that the rear entrance had been broken into."

Gunn looked at Jessica, who shook her head.

"As far as we can tell, the guy is clean. No previous police record. He has no obvious links to the woman."

Gunn looked at Charlie. "CCTV?"

"Nothing, sir," she replied.

"You can't usually take a piss in an alleyway without appearing on a camera in this fucking city, and when you actually need it, you get nothing." Gunn rubbed at the two-day-old stubble on his chin. "What are we missing? Are there any connections between the women?"

"Not that we can see," Jessica replied. "Apart

from the fact that they are female, and that they were brutally murdered, they have nothing in common at all."

Placing the photographs back into the manila folder, he handed it back to Melissa.

"So, what about victim number three?" He asked.

Melissa slid the third folder towards him across the smooth desk. He opened it, and for the third time that afternoon, his lunch threatened to make a re-appearance. Studying the photograph at the front of the folder inquisitively, he asked, "What am I looking at here?"

"That is the remains of Deborah Lewis," Melissa responded.

"What the Hell happened to her?"

"She was found by a load of squatters in an unused flat on Chapeltown Street, near Piccadilly railway station."

Gunn smashed his fist down onto the desk, making everyone jump. "I didn't ask where we *found* her; I asked what had *happened* to her."

"She was found in the bathtub inside the flat. Her body was set alight. The post mortem shows that an accelerant was used, and judging by the scratch marks all over her body, she was most likely conscious when she was burned."

Gunn's mouth gaped. "He burned her alive?"

"From what we can tell, yes. The scratches were most likely from where she tried to extinguish the flames herself. She was the only one of the victims so far that sustained no further injuries."

He pointed to the photograph. "What's all this?"

Melissa swallowed. "Forensics believe that it's the remains of a leather sex mask, sir."

"A … What?"

"It's the charred remains of a gimp mask, sir. The heat from the fire had fused the leather to the woman's face. It was melted into the flesh."

He looked down at the photograph, shook his head.

"Jessica, what did you find?"

"Nothing of any real value, sir. She worked in a sex shop in Cheetham Hill. She lived not far from there. No long-term boyfriend, again, only a few close friends. She hadn't spoken to her parents in a few years."

"What about the fucking squatters? There has to be something. Anyone connected there?"

"We spoke to them but they were reluctant to answer any of our questions. They were worried about the hassle that it could cause them. In the end we had to let them go."

"What about the property?"

"It's just an old flat in a high rise council building, addicts and squatters are always in and out of there. The uniformed guys have to go in now and again to clear them out. We're still having to deal with the fallout of the sixties mentality of building upwards."

Gunn looked at Charlie. "Anything?"

"Not really, the same as the others. No on-going conversations with strangers over social media. It looks like she was paid cash in hand from her employer at the sex shop, so we can't get a detailed look at her outgoings."

"There has to be something," he said.

"Her phone records show that she received a lot of incoming phone calls, so we checked it out with the phone company. It seems that she was running her own sex chat line from her mobile phone."

"What do you mean?"

"Well, she advertised her phone number in the back of a few seedy magazines, as a one to one sexy chat line. Men would ring them up and … you know."

"Get me the details of every single phone number that called her mobile. This could be our only lead."

"Already on it," replied Jessica. "The mobile phone company are working on it as we speak. They said that the records could take up to a couple of days."

He snapped, "Tell them you want those records by tomorrow morning, latest."

"But sir –"

"*Just do it!*"

Pushing his chair out from the desk, he stood up and wiped the sweat from his brow with a swift forearm. He looked around the room slowly at his murder investigation team, the team that assembled personally.

Nobody spoke.

"So we have some fucking deranged psychopath running around Manchester. Butchering, drugging and burning women alive and you're telling me that all we have to go on is one single, weak fucking *lead?*"

Silence filled the room and the team began to look at each other nervously. Nobody spoke a single word. The uncomfortable silence was interrupted by a knock at the office door.

Gunn shook his head, and shouted. "*Come in.*"

A nervous looking police officer entered the room. The DCI recognised her as the young woman who operated the reception desk in the entrance lobby.

"What is it?"

"Sir, I'm sorry to interrupt," she began. "We've just a phone call. There's been another murder."

Killer's Got A Gunn

I leave the engine running to ensure that the cool air is dispersed throughout the seating area of the van. Without it, I would suffocate like a dog left by an irresponsible owner in a car on a hot day. I sit and observe, grabbing a cigarette from the packet resting in the storage compartment to my left. I ignite the tip of the cigarette with the novelty Zippo lighter, adorned with a picture of Zippy from the children's television program, *Rainbow* – a childhood icon that I've grown up with.

I take a long drag from the cigarette, the embers glow a bright orange as I breathe in. Inhaling the smoke deep into my lungs, I savour the taste and immediately feel the relaxing qualities of the nicotine as it begins to work its way into my bloodstream.

I throw the lighter down into the small glove compartment, and slam the door shut. I exhale, and the cabin of the van is filled with a thick plume of grey smoke, clouding my view. I'm unable to open the window because it may draw attention to my location, so I extinguish the cigarette and slam the ash tray shut. It had already served its purpose by calming my nerves and taking the edge off.

I have been returning to this site daily to see whether anything had been disturbed. I always park at a distance, over the road next to the disused service station directly opposite. Nothing has been discovered until today. I know that this location is remote and no longer used, but it's certainly taken long enough to find the body. I was extremely lucky to have been parked up and already keeping a vigil when the police arrived.

Weeks before bringing the whore and leaving her here, I took out the two surveillance cameras that used to look out over the entrance to the industrial estate, ensuring that I wasn't seen coming or going. It's been so long that anybody has used this derelict site that I would be amazed if they were still in operation, I ensured that it was better to be safe than sorry.

I observe the crowd gathering in the distance. Two marked police cars were the first to arrive on the scene. They were the first to speak to the man who must have made the discovery. Ten minutes ago, I watched as he came stumbling out of the front gate of the building and emptied the contents of his stomach all over the pavement. He was fairly young, well dressed in a smart, black suit. Probably a businessman.

I wonder what he was doing here?

A couple of seconds later, he was on his mobile phone and making a call; ringing the police to report the location of the body. A few minutes later, I could hear the sirens approaching in the distance.

A mixture of excitement, dread and exhilaration ran through my entire body as I watched the two police cars speed around the next bend and drive into the industrial estate, their sirens wailing and lights flashing.

I casually observe from the safe distance of my vigil. Two male police officers from each car approach the man and they begin to talk. I can see the man turn and point towards the factory unit, indicating where the body was.

They've found her alright.

Two of the police officers escort the man to one of the vehicles and I watch as he slides into the back seat. It's likely that they will take him off for questioning. It's difficult to tell for sure from this distance but the man looks visibly shaken.

It's hardly surprising considering the state that I left the slut hanging in.

The two officers shut the man inside the car, and

return to the perimeter fence of the factory unit. A moment passes until they are joined by their colleagues who emerge from inside. Judging by the way that they are walking, both men look horrified.

A few moments later and the police cars are joined by the arrival of two, large white vans, both arriving within moments of each other. I watch with delight as three reporters jump out of each van, each with a video camera between them. I must admit, I'm quite impressed with how quickly the two crews arrived on the scene, shortly after I had made my phone calls to them; they were only marginally slower than the boys in blue. I suppose that's what happens when a newspaper office gets a phone call with the location of a murder victim.

I smile as I see them hassling the two police officers standing guard at the gates of the building. They are clearly asking awkward questions, questions that the men are not authorised to answer. I see another of the officers in the distance, quickly winding crime scene tape around the exterior of the entrance to the building, shouting instructions for everyone to stay back.

I check the time on my phone. Now that this body had been discovered, it's only a matter of time. I have things that I need to do, the remainder of today was going to prove to be a busy affair. Luckily, I am already prepared; it's a simple matter of putting my plans into action. However, I don't want to leave just yet.

Not until I see them arrive: The investigation team, my adversaries.

Right on cue, I hear another set of police sirens in the distance as a car comes powering down the street and slides through the entrance to the industrial estate, the back end of the vehicle swerving dangerously, and nearly spinning out altogether, as the driver fights to pull it straight.

The car pulls up, and I feel a spike of hatred coarse through my blood as the door opens and the man steps out; DCI Mark Gunn. He is followed by another three women. I watch as they stand in the bright afternoon sun, looking around them bewildered, wondering where to begin. Gunn looks stressed, it's nothing compared to how he's going to feel soon.

I observe for a few more moments as he speaks to one of the uniformed officers and then directs his team into position to start work.

I put my van into gear, pull off the handbrake and slowly pull away. Nobody pays me the slightest bit of attention as I drive away. Time is of the essence, I have work that needs to be done.

Previous manufacturing premises of Caparo Steel Products

Salford Manchester.

DCI Mark Gunn floored the accelerator on the standard issue Vauxhall Insignia, and desperately weaved the car between the busy queues of traffic throughout the city centre. He opted to take one of the marked police cars from the station. It would make getting through the congestion easier with the use of the sirens. At a little after 16:00, the rush hour traffic had already started to build up, with the regular commuters on their way home.

He pulled into a stream of slow moving cars and created a makeshift lane between the two lines of vehicles. Jessica sat beside him in the passenger seat, riding shotgun, her hands placed out in front of her on the passenger dashboard as if to brace herself ready for impact. Charlie and Melissa sat in the rear of the vehicle in silence, frantically looking around as he steered the car through narrow gaps, the car barely fitting through.

Gunn pulled the vehicle through the oncoming lane of traffic, narrowly missing the cars on either side. As a car in front nearly collided with his front wing, he hammered the horn and stuck his head out of the window, irate.

"Move it. Now. Before I fucking arrest you," he shouted, as the driver begrudgingly pulled his vehicle out of his way.

The rest of the journey consisted the DCI shouting and swearing at oncoming vehicles as he attempted to navigate desperately to their destination. At one point, he actually drove onto the footpath to avoid the heavy traffic ahead. Pedestrians were forced to leap out of the way, as the oncoming police car thundered down the pavement with its sirens blaring, with Gunn's head out of the window, shouting instructions to get out of his way.

The look on his face was one of sheer will and determination. His cheeks had turned a crimson red, and the veins at the side of his temples were beginning to bulge.

"Sir, I really don't think getting us all killed -" Jessica began.

Gunn didn't respond; the look on his face as he snapped around and glared at her was enough to stop her from finishing the sentence. He put his eyes back on the road.

After twenty minutes, he swung the car into the entrance of the dilapidated industrial estate. He located the unit up ahead to the right. A small crowd of people and several uniformed police officers had already gathered outside. He slammed the car into the first available space and jumped out, the engine still running. The other three members of the team jumped out of the car behind him.

Gunn approached the crowd as a young man in a police uniform approached him.

"Status?" he said to the man.

"It's bad," replied the officer. "It's really bad. A man believed to be a real estate developer was looking at the property with a view to developing some contemporary apartments when he found her. We have no idea how long she's been here."

"Where's the man now?" he asked.

The police officer nodded his head towards a figure, seated in the back of one of the other marked police cars. He looked like he was in a world of his own, staring forwards, a vacant look upon his face.

Gunn looked at Jessica. "Jess, go speak to him. Find out everything he knows. I want to know how long he's been considering this property. Who he has been dealing with, any other connections –

everything."

"Yes, sir," Jessica replied, pulling her notebook from the inside pocket of her suit jacket. She approached the car, opened the rear door, and hopped into the car next to the man. He had never seen her approach; he quickly snapped his head round to look at her, startled.

Jessica smiled at him. He was a large man, with dark brown hair in a messy, side parting, combed across his handsome face. He had tanned skin, chiselled features, a strong jaw, and captivating green eyes. His face was wet with perspiration, despite the cool air within the car. Jessica's first impression was that he looked shifty, perhaps a little nervous.

"My name is Jessica Sinnamond," she began. "I'm with the Manchester police. I need to ask you a few questions."

The man looked at her. "You're with the Manchester police? You have a strange accent."

Jessica smiled. "Yes, I moved to England when I was eighteen."

The man looked at Jessica, almost weighing up whether he believed her or not. Jessica flipped open the front cover of her notepad.

"Could I ask your name?"

"Chris, Chris Daniels."

"Thank you, and your age, Chris?"

"I'm forty-three."

She made a scribbled note in her pad. "Chris, I need you to tell me everything that you know about the disused factory, absolutely everything that you can think of, however insignificant, and details of what you found inside."

He looked back at Jessica, his deep green eyes really were captivating, but Jessica couldn't help but think that they held another quality – something almost sinister. The man mused on Jessica's question for a moment, as if considering his response before replying.

"I work for a real estate company called the Daniels Ramsden partnership," he began. "We specialise in buying up old decrepit properties. We buy them way below the market cost and renovate them into luxurious apartments. My business partner lives on the other side of Salford; she told me about this old industrial estate. She figured that it had been derelict for such a long time, and that we could pick it up for next to nothing."

"And have you been dealing with the current owner of the property?"

"No, we haven't got that far with it yet. We've just finished a massive development down south called the Watch Tower, which has been ongoing for the last three years. This has been our first chance to look for a new location."

"So what were you doing on the property when you found the body?"

"I was just taking a look around the site. I wanted to get an idea as to whether the property had any potential."

"So you just happened to be hanging around?" Jessica retorted.

"As I said, I was checking out the premises to see whether it would be worth approaching the current owner," he chuckled. "I can assure you, now, that it's not."

Jessica glared at the man. "Do you think this is funny?"

"Look, I don't want any trouble here, of course not," the man snapped back at her, "but let's face it, it's not every day you discover a dead body that was left to rot in an unused factory. I think I'm doing well so far not to have totally flipped out."

Jessica inspected the man's body language. He was nervous, he was still sweating heavily despite the cool air, and his breathing was becoming erratic.

She nodded. "So how did you get into the unit in the first place, to make the discovery?"

"There was a damaged roller shutter at one end of the building. I just ducked under the gap; it was open to anyone."

Jessica made a few notes in her pad.

"Could I ask your business partner's name?" Jessica asked.

"Of course, it's Julia Ramsden."

The man pulled a business card from the inside pocket of his suit and handed it to Jessica. She noticed that his hand was shaking. She took it from him and inspected the luxurious card with its impressive, black embossed print.

"Please, feel free to give her a call to verify my story," he began, almost pleading. "I can guarantee that she will be more than cooperative."

"Mr Daniels, would you mind hanging around until we complete our initial inspection? I may need to ask you a few more questions."

"I don't want any trouble here," the man repeated, becoming more agitated.

"No," she replied, "it's just a formality."

Jessica opened the car door and walked back over to where the other members of her team were waiting for her. As she walked past, the man looked at her through the car window. Jessica noticed the apprehensive look on his face.

Gunn approached her. "So, who is he?"

"He's a real estate developer," she replied. "He claims that his business partner had sent him here to look for a potential new building development."

Gunn turned and looked at the dilapidated factory. "Here? It's a shit hole."

"That's their niche. They take sub-standard properties and develop them."

"Do you believe him?"

"I'm not sure, sir. There's something off about him, something I just don't trust. I can't put my finger on it."

"Well, for now, he is the only suspect that we have, so he stays put."

Gunn glanced over Jessica's shoulder to the man sitting in the back of the police car. The man noticed him stare and looked away sheepishly.

"Right then, team, we need to do this. We make absolutely no comment to the media. We go in; we check it out as a team."

Walking toward the entrance of the factory unit, a man quickly approached and attempted to shove a video camera in his face.

"DCI Gunn? Can you confirm whether this is the location of another murder victim?"

"No comment."

The man continued. "Sir, can you confirm whether or not you believe that the murders are related?"

Gunn snapped. "Get that fucking camera out of my face."

In a futile attempt to stop the DCI from proceeding, the reporter stood in his way. Gunn grabbed the man by the shoulders and threw him to the ground. He collapsed in a heap on top of his video camera.

"Oh, there we are with the DCI Gunn trademark violence," the fallen man shouted.

Gunn snapped back at him, "Fuck you."

Turning on his heels, he began to storm towards the main entrance of the factory. Police crime-scene tape was stretched across the door.

The disgruntled reporter shouted after him. "Maybe you will need another evidence plant to seal the deal on this one, *Detective Chief Inspector.*"

Gunn stopped on the spot and span round to face the man. He addressed the man, angrily. "What the *fuck* did you say?"

He began quickly walking towards him, when Jessica jumped in his path to intervene. She put her arms out in an attempt to stop him. She pleaded. "Sir, just leave it. He's not worth it."

Gunn hesitated, his breathing deep and laboured, his hands bunched up into fists, ready to fight. He looked over Jessica's shoulder, at the reporter who was now on his feet and beginning to retreat.

He shouted to the man, his voice full of venom. "Get out of my sight."

Jessica turned and breathed a sigh of relief as the man walked away, inspecting the damage done to his camera. As she turned back around, Gunn shoved his face directly into her own. It held a look of pure hatred. "And you," he spat, "if you ever get in my way again, you'll become a part of the fucking problem."

He lashed out with a violent shove that caught her squarely on the shoulder, knocking her off balance. She winced in pain as he turned and stormed back towards the entrance.

He shouted over his shoulder. "Let's go."

The team collected behind him, looking at each other with uncertainty. They tentatively followed his lead into the main entrance of the factory.

As they entered the building, the dim light offered from the overhead strip lights were barely enough for the team to make out the outline of the sickening vision of horror that waited for them in the distance. Even from several metres away, the putrid stench of death hung in the warm air. Gunn winced, pulling a handkerchief from his pocket and holding it up to his face; covering his nose and mouth. He nodded ahead and started to approach, the team slowly followed at his heels.

The naked dead body of a young woman hung

by her wrists from the gantry of the overhead crane, suspended from the hook by steel handcuffs, tight around her wrists. Savage looking wounds peppered her body, her idle head slumped down to her chest, lifeless, and her hair was matted in dried blood and filth.

Charlie was the first to speak. "Holy shit."

Gunn agreed. "Holy shit indeed."

"Melissa, get your arse up here and let's see what we have got," he ordered.

Melissa approached and placed her evidence case on the floor beside the dead woman's feet, ensuring that she avoided the broken glass and congealed bloodstains that had pooled on the concrete. She opened up the case, removing a bundle of evidence bags, and pulled on a pair of latex gloves with a snapping sound.

"We need to know the cause of death," Gunn said.

Melissa approached the dead body of the woman carefully, watching where she stepped. In her career on the force, she had seen many sickening sights; this was up there with the worst of them. She inspected the scene. The woman's brown hair hung down from her head, obscuring her face. Her wrists had turned deep shades of purple and black. Small cuts from the metal had opened up on her wrists, the bruises ruptured from where her body weight had hung, suspended from the cuffs. Her torso was a bloody mess; it had been cut open below her ribcage, and her abdomen looked distorted and completely out of shape.

Melissa run her fingers over one of the lacerations on the dead woman's body. She took a sharp intake of breath.

"Sir," she began. "Her ribs have been snapped."

"Snapped?" replied Mark. "How the fuck do you snap someone's ribs?"

"I have no idea. He must have used some kind of wrenching device. If she was still alive, this poor woman must have been in complete agony."

Melissa followed the trail of dried blood that ran down the dead girl's legs, it pooled on the concrete floor at her feet. She dipped her gloved finger into the deep crimson puddle, it was still sticky to the touch. She grabbed a small penlight from inside her kit back to try to find the source of the bleeding. Running the small beam from the penlight up the woman's thighs, she spotted the wound between the woman's legs. She gasped, placing her hand over her mouth.

"Jesus, sir, we're dealing with one sick bastard here."

"What is it?"

"He's cut her open."

"I can see that, she's covered in cuts."

Melissa turned to face Mark, and then shone the beam of the penlight at the dead woman's exposed crotch. "No, sir. He's *cut* her open."

"Fucking hell," Gunn replied in shock. "Would you say that was the cause of death?"

"It's difficult to say for certain, there's so much blood. We're going to need a post mortem to be sure."

Looking around, Melissa spotted a large shard of jagged glass on the floor near to the woman's bare feet. Bending down, she picked it up. Bits of dried blood and gore clung to the tip and spooled down the jagged sides. She withheld the sudden urge to vomit.

Gunn stepped forward. "What have you got?"

Melissa stood and turned, the large piece of broken, filthy glass held out in her shaking hand towards the DCI. Gunn inspected the glass for a few seconds with a look of complete confusion, until it suddenly dawned on him.

"You have got to be *fucking* kidding me?"

"No, sir. It looks like he used the glass to cut the

poor woman open."

Behind him, Jessica lurched forward and emptied the contents of her stomach onto the concrete floor between her feet, with a massive splash.

Gunn turned to face Charlie. "Go and take a good look around the premises. See if there are any working CCTV cameras anywhere. If you find any, I want copies of the tapes from the last two months. Jessica, go and wait outside."

Both of the women nodded, and responded in unison. "Yes, sir." Jessica wiped the remaining vomit from her mouth with her sleeve. Both women turned and began to retreat towards the main entrance.

He turned to Melissa. "Not a very strong stomach for a so-called Maniac Cop."

"Maybe she's never witnessed a body that's been pitilessly murdered before," she replied.

Gunn ignored her comment. "What else do we have?"

Melissa shone the penlight down near the girl's feet as something small and metallic reflected in the beam. Melissa bent down to inspect the item. Carefully, she picked it up between her thumb and index finger. She brought the item close to her face to try to get a better look.

"What have you got?"

She frowned. "I'm not sure. It looks like some sort of jewellery."

He nodded towards the body. "Is it from her?"

"I can't be sure."

"Bag it up. It may be evidence."

Melissa inspected the small metal item. It looked like one of the fashionable ring accessories for piercings worn through the nose or eyebrow. She opened an evidence bag and dropped the item inside. She turned back to the girl, unable to see her face or ears through her brown hair.

"Sir, I think it's a facial piercing. I'm going to check."

"Go ahead," he replied. "Be careful."

Melissa gently clutched the girls head carefully in her hands. The hair was sticky and filthy with a mixture of blood, moisture and grime. She slowly lifted the head, it was heavier than she had expected. She continued to lift slowly until the dead woman's face was staring straight back at her. Her eyes were wide open with an expression of utter fright. Melissa noticed that above her eye was a tear in the flesh, indicating that the piercing formerly resided in the eyebrow.

The woman's mouth was a total mess. Disturbed by the sudden movement, a thick stream of dark red and black liquid sluiced from the orifice, splashing down her chin and neck. Without warning, the lower section of the woman's face fell open at an un-natural angle. Melissa yelped, snapping her own head back in shock, but managed to retain her grip on the sides of the head, as the whole bottom portion of the woman's jaw hung limp for a few seconds. Melissa looked on in complete bewilderment, unable to move. After a stomach-turning, shredding sound, the woman's jaw peeled from her face and plunged towards the floor, landing with a heavy thump on Melissa's left foot.

Melissa let go of the head in panic; it fell awkwardly back down to its previous position with a squelching sound. She turned to Gunn with a mortified look on her face.

"I think we have just found the cause of death, sir," she said.

Gunn knelt down on one knee, carefully avoiding the broken glass and congealed pools of blood. He stared in awe at the severed section of the woman's jaw. It looked like a large portion of uncooked steak with sharp remains of ragged bone protruding from the discoloured flesh.

"What the fuck am I looking at here, Melissa? How the hell has he ripped her face apart?"

"It's her jaw, sir."

"Her jaw?"

"Yes. Somehow, the killer managed to separate the lower section of her mouth from the rest of her face. Judging by the look in the woman's eyes, she was still conscious when it happened."

Gunn stared for a moment at the piece of the woman's dissevered face on the filthy factory floor; surrounded by dozens of dried pools of blood that must have sprayed from the woman's mouth during her ordeal, his mind trying to comprehend what Melissa had just told him. Still kneeling, he turned and looked up at her.

"We've got a total fucking psychopath on our hands here."

"I can't argue with that," Melissa agreed.

"Right, let's get this area sealed off properly. I'll get the medical crew in here - not that they can do a great deal for her. I want her out of here and a post mortem done as quickly as possible. I want this woman identified."

Melissa carefully picked up the piece of the woman's face and dropped it into another plastic evidence bag. She packed away the other items that she had collected from the scene, placed them into her case and re-latched it shut.

Both officers walked back in complete silence to the main entrance of the factory, ensuring that, as they walked, they didn't come into contact with anything that was considered evidence. The crowd of people outside the building had increased; he called over two police officers and the members of the medical team. He gave them instructions to remove the body from the crane and have it transported by ambulance, back to a coroner for the post mortem.

He turned to Melissa. "Go with them. Report back to me as soon as you have anything."

He walked towards Jessica, who was leaning over the front wing of a parked police car. She stood up straight as she spotted him approaching.

"I'm sorry about that, sir. It was just a little unexpected."

"Don't worry about it," he began. "You wouldn't have wanted to wait around for the encore."

Jessica frowned. "How do you mean?"

He looked round and spotted Charlie walking quickly towards him. "I'll fill you in later. What did you find, Charlie?"

Her face said it all. "Nothing, sir. Not one single CCTV camera in the vicinity. The whole estate has been derelict for years. No security guards and no surveillance. It's probably a hive for the homeless."

"Find the land owners," he said to Charlie. "I want to know exactly what they know, who has access, everything."

Gunn turned to Jessica. "This is turning out to be a fucking nightmare."

Jessica nodded. "What do we do now, sir?"

"I'm going to have to speak to the media and put out a press release. We need to try and stop this from becoming a media frenzy and a public alarm. But first, there's something I need to do."

"What's that?"

Gunn glanced over Jessica's shoulder at the man sat in the back of the police car. The man looked up and their eyes met. Even from a distance, the DCI could see that the man had a look of pure anxiety on his face.

Jessica looked at Gunn as he nodded towards the man in the car. "I want to speak to him."

Greater Manchester Police Station

Interrogation Room

Sweat was beginning to pool on his brow. The overhead fan made Chris Daniels' head feel cold.

How long had he been waiting now?
An hour? Two?

"This is what I get for trying to do the right thing."

Chris said it aloud, no longer just thinking it. He noticed two CCTV cameras in the corner of the room. He felt sure that he was being monitored at this very moment, and he wanted to show these pigs that he hadn't done anything wrong.

"Hello?" he shouted. "You can't just leave me here. I haven't done anything wrong."

The door opened and the large officer that Chris had seen back at the warehouse entered. He stood up; ready to argue about his current situation, and his release.

"Sit down," DCI Gunn said, sternly.

Chris sat back in his seat like a naughty pupil being chastised by his teacher.

"Listen," Chris said. "I haven't done anything wrong. I did the right thing, I saw the body and I called the police. And now, you guys are punishing me for it. It's not fair. This isn't how it's supposed to work. I haven't been able to call home. Work are going to think I've just left the site without checking in."

Gunn sat with his arms folded across his chest, his jaw clenched tight. Chris looked at him waiting for a response.

"Well?" Chris asked. "What the hell is going on? Do I get to go home now, or what?"

"Have you finished?" Gunn asked.

"What?"

"Have you finished?" Gunn repeated, his eyes

unblinking, boring into Chris'.

"Um, yeah um I guess," Chris began to mumble.

Gunn nodded. "Right then. I'm *so* sorry that we've been a minor inconvenience to you today. I wish we could have gotten to you sooner so that you could have had a longer lunch break. I've been a bit preoccupied picking that poor girl's jawbone up from the *bloody floor!*"

Chris shuffled in his seat, once again resembling a pupil under verbal assault.

"Now." Gunn looked at the piece of paper in front of him. "Mr Daniels. Can you tell me what you were doing at that warehouse today?"

"I've already told you what I was doing there today. I told that American girl twice. Once at the warehouse and once here."

"Yes, but you haven't told me, have you?"

"Look. I haven't done anything wrong! I shouldn't be getting treated like a criminal here."

"I assure you, Mr Daniels, if I was to treat you like a criminal, then you would certainly know about it. I'm not so nice to all of our guests." Gunn smiled. "Or would you like me to call a solicitor for you?"

"Guests? Are you taking the fucking *piss!*"

"Watch your language, Mr Daniels."

"No. You can't just leave me in here for bloody hours and then come in and start patronising me and…"

"Who is Stacy Bagot?" Gunn interrupted.

"What?" Chris asked. He suddenly felt uncomfortable. His head shined sleek with perspiration.

"Sorry, you probably couldn't hear me with all your shouting. Perhaps if we talk nicely now, we won't have to repeat ourselves?"

"I'm sorry. I'm just tired, and I would like to go home," Chris whined.

"And you will, Mr Daniels, but first, you need to

tell me about Stacy Bagot."

"She's just a woman I used to work with," Chris mumbled.

"I'm sorry. I didn't quite get that."

"She's just a woman I used to work with," Chris repeated.

"Just a woman you used to work with. Is there nothing else that you would like to tell me about Ms Bagot?"

"No. She's just a woman I used…"

"Do you think I'm an *idiot*, Mr Daniels?" Gunn interrupted.

"What?"

"Right, I'm not stupid and you're not fucking deaf, so let's stop with all this repeating questions bullshit, the mumbling and the lying, okay? If you want, we can play this game, but you seem to be in a rush to get home, and I have a feeling that unless we stop messing about, both you and I are in for a long night."

"Okay, okay, Im sorry."

"Okay. Now, Ms Bagot was a woman that you worked with and raped prior to her dismissal from your company. Is that correct?"

"*No!*" Chris argued. "I was never charged for her rape."

"I never said that you were *charged* for her rape, Mr Daniels. What I asked was simple. Is she a woman that you raped prior to her dismissal from your company? Whether you were officially charged or not is completely irrelevant to me."

"You can't accuse me of that. I fought that case and I won. You can't just go around calling me a rapist." Chris stood up from his chair.

"Sit down, Mr Daniels."

"No."

"*Sit down!*" Gunn roared.

Chris plonked back down to his seat.

"Listen to me. I'm not *accusing* you of anything,

but I can tell you this. I have been in this game for a very long time. Criminals, whether convicted or not, acquire a certain look over the years. Call it a scar if you will, or an affliction. I don't know the science behind it, maybe it's the stress of continually looking over their shoulder. Maybe it's just some weird justice from God that they have to carry that mark for life. You see, not everyone can see that mark. You have to be trained to see it. I can spot a criminal in a crowded room. He carries more weight than the rest of the people. If you carry that weight for too long then it starts to show. Convicted or not, Mr Daniels, I say that you are a criminal. A non-convicted *rapist.* If that's how you want to say it. But what I see is a man guilty of doing harm to a woman. And where do I find this man? With the body of another woman. Only this time it looks like he's upped his game." Gunn sat back and folded his arms once more. Then he flashed a smile.

Chris stared down at the table, scratched the back of his neck and started to pull at his shirt collar. "I, I…"

"Go on." Gunn smiled.

"I'm not saying another word without a solicitor."

"Fine." Gunn stood up and left the room.

Manchester Police Station

The door flew open, shattering the silence with a loud bang as the handle smacked into the wall, leaving a crumpled hole. Melissa jumped, spilling some of her coffee down her shirt.

"Shit," she cursed.

Gunn stormed across the room muttering something under his breath. Melissa sidled behind him, trying to grab a paper towel to wipe her shirt, but at the same time avoid getting in his way.

"*Lason!*" Gunn spat.

Melissa stopped what she was doing immediately, and stood with her arms by her sides. She felt like a soldier lining up for duty.

"Yes, sir?"

"Give me something."

"Um." She looked around for inspiration. "Coffee, sir?"

Gunn looked at her as though she had two heads.

"No, I don't want coffee. Give me something from the crime scene." He looked across the room to see Charlie busily typing away on the laptop. "Where's the rookie?"

"You mean Jessica, sir? She stuck around at the warehouse for a bit. She's going to see if she can find any more witnesses. Any drivers or workmen who may pass through the area regularly, other people that might have seen something."

"Okay, okay, good stuff." He nodded. "Did you find anything of use at the crime scene? Anything which can nail that cocky bastard I've got sat in the other room?"

"Besides the girl we've got nothing, boss. But…"

"*Nothing!*" Gunn interrupted. "How can this fucker continuously leave us with nothing? He must have left something behind. No one can clean a crime scene so thoroughly."

He paced across the room and leaned on Charlie's desk. She didn't even look up from her screen. She just continued to type.

"Tell me that you've found something," he said.

"Nothing yet. I've been going through the local CCTV footage. There's plenty of traffic passing through that area, but there are no cameras covering the turn off to the warehouse road. I'm scanning the footage to see if I can spot a car with the girl in, but as I say, there is a lot of traffic going through that route. It's like finding a needle in a haystack." Charlie turned her attention back to the screen and continued to type.

"Have we got any idea who this girl is yet? Have you checked missing persons?"

"Well," Melissa said. "That's what I was trying to say. We've identified the girl as a Julie Shields. A tourist who went missing last week."

"A tourist?" Gunn slammed his hands down in despair. "This is all we need. The press are going to be all over this."

"Well, we don't have a one hundred percent confirmation yet, but it's looking highly likely. The girl we found had a birthmark on her left hip in the shape of a heart. She's six foot with brown hair. Plus, she's the only woman on the missing persons list that matches that description."

"Has her family been notified?"

"Well, we've contacted her husband and asked if he can come to identify the body. It was him who listed the birthmark as a distinguishing feature when he reported her missing."

"Okay, I want to try and keep this as quiet as possible. The press doesn't need to know that we've identified her yet. God knows, we've never identified anyone that quickly before."

"*Thank you*," Charlie shouted.

Gunn turned to look at her, confused.

"She's the one who identified the victim," Melissa clarified. "She said that it would be some kind of record and that no one will have identified anyone so quickly."

"Oh, well, I'm glad that this is all fun and games for you. If you want to start breaking records then get moving and find out who the bloody killer is."

"I'm trying, I'm…" Charlie turned around to meet Gunn's stare. "On it, boss." She turned back to the computer.

Gunn walked to the window and then stood staring at the grey sky. He was mumbling something to himself again.

"What's that, boss?" Melissa asked.

"What?" Gunn turned around. "Oh sorry. I'm just thinking aloud. Right this guy's solicitor is probably going to be here at any minute. I could do with someone coming in to interview him properly with me. I can't keep my tongue with those smarmy no comment bastards in the room."

"I'll come in with you."

"No, no. I want you to go back to the warehouse and have another look to see if there's anything we've missed. You can help Jessica out. There has to be something that can help us, even if it's just a hair or a finger nail. Anything at all."

"So, Charlie?"

"No, she needs to keep going through that footage. Actually, get Jessica on the phone. I want her back here, now."

The door opened and Jessica entered.

"Oh, speak of the devil," Gunn said.

Jessica looked flustered, a mild panic filled her eyes. Everyone in the room seemed to sense it and they stopped what they were doing.

"What is it?" Melissa asked.

"They've found another," Jessica said. "The call has just come in."

"Two in one day?" Gunn marched across the room. "You've got to be shitting me. Charlie, go and put Mr Daniels in a holding cell for now. If this one is fresh, then it looks like we've got the wrong guy, but I don't want to let him go just yet. Just in case."

Melissa and Jessica now stood side-by-side, awaiting instruction.

"You two with me. We need to go and see what we're dealing with here."

Gunn left the room, and his team followed.

Burnage

Manchester Suburbs.

Gunn parked the car outside the grocers. The row of shops was on a busy road, two lanes in each direction, and linking straight onto the M56. It wasn't exactly a discreet location.

"Don't tell me he's dumped her in the middle of the shop," Gunn said.

"No, it's in the flat upstairs, sir," the uniformed officer who met Gunn responded. "And it's a mess. I've never seen anything like it. I… I"

"Alright, son. You just stay out here and keep an eye out for any witnesses. And don't let anyone in without authorisation, okay?"

"Okay, thanks, sir."

Gunn walked side by side with Melissa and Jessica into the shop. He scanned the place as they proceeded through. Nothing looked untoward. There was no mess, or any sign of a break in.

"Is this the only way in?" he asked.

"No, apparently there is an entrance through an alley at the back as well," Jessica answered.

"Right, Melissa. You go around the back and get a good look at that entrance. I don't want anyone messing it up. Check the gate, the alley, fuck, even check the puddles on the floor. Anything at all to nail this bastard."

"On it." Melissa walked back through the front door to the shop and made her way around the back. Gunn and Jessica carried on through the store. They went through a door which led into a small staff room. Nothing much to see in there, just a sink, a kettle and a fridge. Again, there was no mess or sign of disruption.

A door led from the staff room into a back yard.

To the right was another door, it was already open. Jessica checked the lock on the way in. No sign of forced entry. Gunn shoved passed her and made his way up the stairs.

"Oh, *Christ!*" Gunn shouted. "This has to be the same guy, Jessica get up here!"

Jessica rushed up the stairs and into the room where Gunn was waiting. She gasped at the sight in front of her. The victim lay with her head upside down resting on the floor. The rest of her body arched up onto the bed, like she had frozen mid-fall. Her hair was drenched red with blood that had poured from her slit throat. Her eyes held a wide stare of death. Jessica couldn't help but stop and stare at them for a moment. Then she scanned the rest of the body. Her nipples had been cut off; two large holes remained in the breasts, circled with multiple shades of red where the blood had run. She looked further along the body, there were no marks on the stomach, but she could see something large sticking out from underneath her.

"What's that underneath…"

"It's a chair leg," Gunn interrupted. "And it's not underneath her, it's *in* her."

"Oh my God," Jessica gasped. "Why would anyone do that?"

"Exactly, I've not seen anything this brutal for years, not until today. I've had two of them, and it's more than enough." He gritted his teeth. "We really need to catch this guy."

Melissa entered the room. She stood for a long moment staring at the body, then composed herself. "No sign of anything unusual from the back entrance."

"Nothing at all?"

"Nothing, even the alley gate lock was intact."

"Okay, what do we know about the victim?" Gunn asked.

"Shop is owned by a Donna Lockley, but she's away on holiday right now. The flat is rented by yours truly here." Jessica gestured to the body. "Her name is Gina Hawkins. Judging by the clothes in here there's a boyfriend as well, but we don't have any details on him, yet."

Gunn paced the room, stopping every now and then to stare at a specific point, looking for inspiration. Jessica stood almost in a trance, staring at the body, and Melissa had started to look for anything in the room that could help them identify the suspect.

"How could anyone do something like that?" Jessica whispered.

"It's best not to stare too long," Gunn said. "Otherwise, you will be seeing her in your sleep."

"I don't think I'll be able to forget those eyes."

"You have to switch off, it's just part of the job. You…"

"*Got it!*" Melissa shouted.

"What is it?" Gunn asked, unable to hide the excitement in his voice.

"Our victim was thinking of moving." Melissa held up a flyer in her hand. The header said *Daniels Ramsden Partnership.*

"We've got him," Gunn called. "*We've got him!* Come on, let's get back to the station now. I can't wait to see this bastard's face."

The team exited the crime scene, leaving the retrieval of evidence, and the body, to the CSI and clean up squad. Gunn couldn't contain his grin for the whole drive back. He was beginning to think that he was never going to catch this guy, and now they had him. Now he could have a decent night's sleep for the first time in weeks.

They entered the station like celebrities, with huge smirks on their faces and a strut in their stride. Charlie rushed to the door to greet them.

"Sir, I need to tell you…"

"Hang on a second, Charlie. I'm need to tell Mr Daniels that he's under arrest for murder."

"For the warehouse girl?"

"No, for all of them. We've just found his paperwork at Gina Hawkins' flat."

"But that's just it. Gina Hawkins' boyfriend, John Barton, has just walked through the door and confessed to her murder. He's in the holding cell, waiting to be interviewed."

"Are you fucking kidding me?"

"No. Apparently, he caught her cheating and he killed her. He said he wanted to turn himself in before he found out who the other guy is, and killed him too."

"But we found the flyer from the real estate guy?"

"That's all part of Barton's confession. He was so upset because they were planning to move in together. I hate to say it, boss, but I think the flyer may have just been a coincidence."

"Well, it doesn't put Daniels in the clear, and for all we know, this Barton guy may have been the one who killed the other girls as well."

"I hate to say it, but Barton was on holiday when the first two victims were killed. And we're waiting on confirmation, but Daniels is saying that he was away on business as well. If he can back that up, then we're back to square one."

Gunn walked back out of the door without saying a word to the rest of the team. Jessica moved to follow him.

"Wait," Charlie said.

Jessica frowned. "But…"

"Just give him a minute, he'll be back. He just needs to vent for a second. He does this every now and then."

Gunn stormed back into the station, throwing the doors open in front of him.

"Right, Charlie. You get back on those surveillance cameras, we're not giving up until we find something. Melissa and Jessica, I want you to both go back to each crime scene. I know you've checked them for evidence, but now I want you to sit back and look at them as a location. Are there any similarities at all. Anything that can even give us a hint to the personality of the killer."

"And where will you be, sir?" Jessica asked.

"I'm going to go speak to this Barton guy."

Killer's Got A Gunn

I sit in my van parked at the rear of Manchester police station, ensuring that I don't park too closely. I don't want to be spotted. Following my initial preparations, after they discovered the body at the Industrial units, I doubled back and came straight to the station. I have to be clear on their movements, and try to figure out how much they know.

It's been manic here all day; vehicles coming and going ever since I arrived. Everything is in place, ready for the next phase; I just need to keep my eye on where the investigation team are going. I can't have them getting too close, or the most unlikely case; lucky.

I stay in position as more vehicles drive in and out of the car park. I check the time on my phone. Glancing up from the screen, I see her standing in the car park. The blonde-haired American woman from the investigation team. She's standing near the exit of the car park, talking with another uniformed officer. After a few moments of discussion, she jumps into her own vehicle and I watch as the car pulls out of the car park. I put my car into gear and pull out, cautiously following her, ensuring that I keep a relatively safe distance. There are two cars between hers and my van.

Where are you off to, blondie?

I continue to follow her at a distance, as she turns left onto Craigsland Avenue. The afternoon traffic had already began to mount up in the streets, the one thing that I always hated about this city. We wait for a few minutes in a line of traffic at the busy junction, before she turns left again into Halliford Road.

After another stop-start journey down a narrow causeway, she indicates left onto Thorpe Road. Another right turn will bring us out onto Oldham Road.

Of course, I know where she's going.

She's heading back to the flats in Piccadilly.

At this time of day, the ten-minute journey will take nearer to thirty.

I need to get there before she does. I indicate and spin the van around so that I'm travelling in the opposite direction. Flooring the accelerator, I head back along the road once again. I throw the van around the next bend and into the side street.

I know a shortcut.

Disused flats

Piccadilly

Jessica pulled her car into the last remaining space at the rear of the apartment complex, putting the gear into neutral. Routing through her glove box, she pushed the packets of tissues and mints aside, until she found the two items she was searching for; her torch and her pepper spray. She could hardly believe that, in a job where they were chasing down a psychopathic murderer, the English police weren't allowed to carry fire arms for protection.

Retrieving the pepper spray from the glove compartment, she tucked it away into the pocket on the inside of her jacket. She clicked the button on the top of the torch to check that it had sufficient battery life. The beam shot out across the inside of the car. Grabbing her plastic evidence box from the back seat in one hand, and the torch in the other, she confirmed that she had what she needed, and stepped out of her car. Locking the doors behind her with her key fob, she then snapped on a pair of rubber examination gloves.

As she exited the car, the late afternoon sun shone down on her, intensified by the dark-coloured trouser suit that Jessica was wearing. She immediately began to sweat. Removing her sunglasses and placing them into her pocket, she wiped away the first beads of moisture from her brow with the back of her sleeve.

A hundred yards away in the distance, the audible sound of a camera shutter clicking twice, could be heard inside a vehicle.

Jessica began to walk along the perimeter of the car park, scanning the floor for potential clues; anything that they may have already missed. Kicking her shoes gently through the remains of litter that had collected in the gutters; mainly empty drinks cans, cigarette packets, and faded takeaway flyers. She found nothing.

She continued along the kerbside, towards the car where the figure with the camera sat. After taking another few pictures, Jessica neared, now less than thirty yards away. The observer ducked down into the foot well of the vehicle to ensure they weren't spotted.

Jessica turned and looked up at the dilapidated building; several of the windows from the lower floors were smashed, and nobody had bothered to fix them. There was nothing particularly remarkable or unique about the structure, just another of the many decrepit buildings that blended into the background, that created the grey concrete monstrosity of Manchester's inner city.

Encircling around to the rear of the building, she pulled her mobile phone from her pocket, and checked the notes application where she had made a note of the code for the access door. Punching the code C4675B into the metal access security device, she ducked underneath the yellow crime scene tape, and made her way into the apartment structure.

Inside the building, the air was stale and the heat was stifling from the afternoon sun. Dust particles danced in the air as she switched on her torch, and invaded her airways as she breathed in, nearly making her sneeze. Once again, with the intensity of the confined heat, she began to sweat.

In front of her stood a large, rectangular concrete staircase. To her right was an old metal door that acted as the access point for the lift shaft. Graffiti adorned the scuffed doors, cheap spray paint and black marker pen, crudely drawn with names of gang members or local youths who considered themselves somewhat of a celebrity. The whole building was a hovel, cracked paint and plaster hung from the walls, there was a stagnant aroma of urine and faeces that hung in the air.

She took the forward route, deciding that the stairs were probably the more sensible course of action. Shining the beam of her torch down onto the steps, she began searching for clues, anything at all. Broken glass crunched underneath her feet as she ascended the stairwell, one cautious step at a time.

Keeping the beam of her torch low, she continued to rummage – she found nothing. As she made her way up to the second floor, the heat increased and her senses picked up the remains of the fire from where the police had recovered the body of the third victim; Deborah Lewis.

Opening the doorway from the main stairwell, there was a welcome breeze, the cooler air brushed against Jessica's face as she walked through onto the landing. She continued her way down the corridor, shining the beam from her torch down amongst the rubble that had collected on the floor. After a few moments of searching, something metallic reflected in the beam of light.

Kneeling down on one knee, Jessica put the torch down on the floor so that the beam shone onto the item. Pulling a pen from her inside pocket, she poked around in the debris to uncover the object. Jessica took a sharp intake of breath as she realised what the item was. Pulling a plastic evidence bag from her back pocket, she shook it out ready and picked the item up with the tip of the pen. Retrieving the torch from where she had placed it on the ground, she held up the evidence bag and shined the light at it. Staring back at her was a pair of hinged metal handcuffs. They looked just like her own, definitely police issue.

Had someone from the evidence team dropped them?

She pulled her mobile from her pocket and clicked the display to make a call. The digital display showed the SOS logo. No signal.

Shit.

She stood up, holding the evidence bag containing the handcuffs in one hand, and the torch in the other, and slowly walked forwards. She dropped the cuffs into her plastic evidence box. Continuing down the hall, she reached the third door on the left hand side, and ripped away the police tape, pushing her shoulder against the door. After a little resistance, the door gave way and Jessica sprawled into the apartment. The overpowering, putrid stench of burned flesh and chemicals hung in the air. She somehow resisted the urge to vomit, and buried her nose in the crease of her elbow. The overbearing stench began to make her eyes stream.

She continued into the main area of the apartment, which contained no items of furniture or decoration. She shone the beam of her torch around the perimeter of the floor, searching for any items that may have been discarded or dropped. In the far corner of the living area, she found a small wooden table that contained a few items - two used syringes and a bent, metal spoon. Pulling another plastic bag from her pocket, she carefully placed the items into the bag, ensuring that she didn't prick her fingers or hands, then sealed up the bag and dropped it into her evidence box, along with the handcuffs.

After another quick scan of the room with the torch, she began moving towards the bathroom. As she opened the door, the smell became overpowering and caused her to retch, almost emptying her stomach once again.

The stench of scorched flesh and death hung in the air. Jessica continued forwards, slowly with the torch, shining the beam into the bathtub. Someone had removed the charred and blackened remains, just leaving a few flakes of burnt residue and ash, and a scorched tub.

Despite the fire being intense enough to burn a body, it had remained localised due to the accelerant that was poured directly onto the victim's body, before she was set alight. Jessica shined the torch up at the ceiling; the paint had blackened and blistered from where the smoke and intense heat had climbed and attacked its surface.

Turning round, Jessica shone the beam from the torch over towards the sink. Hung down one side of the bowl was a single blonde hair. Using a pair of tweezers, she carefully collected the hair and placed it into another evidence bag when suddenly, the sound of something smashing out in the hallway made her jump.

She quickly grabbed the pepper spray from her inside pocket and held it out in front of her face. She moved out into the main living area and shouted. "Who's there? This is the police."

No response.

She shouted again. "Give yourself up, I'm armed."

Again, no response.

She moved forwards slowly, shining the beam around frantically, searching. She spotted nothing. Her heart was thundering in her chest, the hot air and smell of decay made her breathing laboured and difficult. Her hair clung to her head with sweat.

Approaching the main entrance to the apartment that led out onto the focal hallway, she called out once again. "Hello, is anyone there? This is the police."

Silence.

Taking a deep breath, she moved out into the hallway, shining the light down to the right from the way she had approached. She saw nothing. As she spun back around, she barely had time to spot the large figure that hurtled towards her. A solid punch connected with her chin, causing her to spin sideways, and hit the floor with a heavy thump. The torch dropped from her hand and she groaned in pain. The room began to spin as she saw her attacker quickly disappear down the corridor, and through the main entrance with her evidence box. She heard footsteps falling as they disappeared down the stairs.

She was losing consciousness. Then, there was nothing.

The figure in the car outside the building remained, patiently observing as the outline of a filthy tramp emerged from the side of the building, stumbling and running towards the car, clutching the evidence box.

The tramp walked up to the driver door, and held up the box. "You said fifty quid, right?"

Without saying a word, the stranger held out the wad of crisp notes. The tramp quickly handed over the box, and snatched the money. Seconds later, he had disappeared from sight down an alleyway. The stranger remained, observing.

Four minutes later, the police officer appeared in the car park. She looked distressed, agitated. She span around frantically on the spot, searching for the tramp who had just disappeared up the alley. After a few seconds, she unlocked her car and climbed back in. The observer smiled and took a few more pictures, as Jessica put the phone to her ear.

Back in her car, Jessica dialled Gunn's mobile number. She touched her jaw from where she had been punched, wincing in pain. The call went straight through to his answer machine. She dialled again, this time calling through to the police station. After the fourth ring, someone answered her call.

"Hello, Greater Manchester Police Station, how

can I help?"

"Hey, it's Sinnamond. I'm trying to get hold of Gunn. I'm across at the derelict flats at Piccadilly, I fucked up. I think I had our man, and I let him get away."

The officer on the other end of the phone remained silent for a second, before responding. "Jess, I think you had better get back here. Gunn's been in with the suspect while you've been out. He's confessed to the murders."

"Who, Daniels?"

"Yes, you'd better get back here."

"I'm on my way."

Without saying goodbye, she terminated the call and quickly started up the engine of her car. The observer watched as she screeched dangerously out of the car park and hurtled away at speed. Then, they started their own car and drove off in the opposite direction.

Derelict Building – Previously

One Stop Local Store – Moss Side Manchester

Melissa drove her car down the main Claremont Road, through the suburb of Moss Side. She wiped the sweat from her brow with the back of her hand. Being born and raised in Arizona meant that she was used to the prickly heat, and being stuck in a standard issue police car in the middle of summer, with broken air conditioning, came a very close second to that sort of hell.

Driving through the centre of one of the roughest areas of Manchester, she decided to sacrifice her comfort for the sake of safety, and left her window wound right up, and the doors locked. As she drove through the first couple of streets, two small gangs of youths in baseball caps stopped and stared as she passed. It was almost as if they sensed that she was an outsider.

As she progressed further into the housing estate, young children that should have been at school were playing in the gardens at the front of their houses, whilst their mothers were stood chatting away with their neighbours and smoking, leaving them free to do as they pleased.

A couple of doors down, four young men were stood topless in the street, drinking beer straight from the can while laughing at two dogs, humping on the footpath in clear view of the road. As she rounded the next corner, she was surprised to see a horse being led down the footpath by a child no older than twelve-years-old. She had to steer the car, narrowly avoiding a collision with the animal as it reared and kicked, and began to bolt from the child.

She slowed the vehicle as she turned into Cowesby Street, and located the row of derelict shops up ahead on the right hand side of the road. It was a line of four neglected buildings; the first building displayed a sign for an old launderette, the shop in the middle was an old fish and chip takeaway, and the final building was the old local store. The shutters were pulled shut indefinitely, and were now decorated with various forms of spray paint and graffiti. Several of the windows on the front of the building had been smashed, but looters were unable to access the store because of bars that were secured over the windows. Several of the red, slated tiles on the roof were either missing or broken.

The main thing that Melissa noticed was how quiet this street was, compared to the rest of the streets that she had just driven down. As there were no houses, it was definitely more secluded, and there were less people milling about.

The perfect place to bring Vicky Stuart to be murdered.

Pulling the car around the corner of the last shop, she parked up in a small space next to a black van at the rear of the row of shops, a thoroughfare originally intended for loading or unloading. She turned off the engine and stepped from the vehicle. A concrete stairwell ran up the rear of the local store and ran across all three of the buildings, as if they all shared a communal balcony. Each doorway was covered with a metal security door to prevent looters.

She walked over to the black van, her suspicion aroused, as the shops were no longer in use. She had a look around the outside; it was a standard Transit van, with no rear windows. She tried the doors - locked. Moving around to the front of the vehicle, she peered through the driver's window. There was nothing obvious on display to cause any reason for concern. She tried the door; once again, it was locked. Pulling a notepad from her back pocket, she took a note of the vehicle registration number to check later, just to be on the safe side.

As far as you know, it's been parked here for weeks.

She put away the notebook and went into the boot of her car, collecting her evidence box. She pulled on a pair of latex gloves, and turned on her torch. As she ascended the stairs, she had the strange sensation that she was being watched. She spun around, and inspected the loading bay from the raised elevation of the balcony. She saw nobody, she heard nothing; it was eerily quiet.

Turning, she took the keys from her pocket and fumbled with the bunch, trying each one in the lock until she found the one that fitted. She turned the key and heard the sound of metal clicking as the door unlocked, and the metal security door dropped on its hinges by a few inches.

Swinging the door aside, she stepped over the metal ledge into the property, immediately hit by the penetrating, contained heat. Her stomach turned as the decomposed stench of death hit her. She waited by the main entrance for a few seconds, taking in large gulps of air, completely filling her lungs before advancing any further.

Shining the torch around, she followed the corridor around to the left. Using the overpowering smell of decay as a guide, she continued forward. On both sides of the main corridor were stacked boxes and old tea chests. When she reached the landing, she found a bannister and a stairway that ran down to another security door.

Presumably to the shop.

She opened the door to the first bedroom, and inspected it. The space was very bare, no furniture, nothing stored, just damp walls in garish green and brown wallpaper, and bare floorboards. She shone the beam down to the perimeter of the floor, searching between the boards for any evidence; she found nothing.

Backing out of the room, she closed the door behind her and slowly made her way towards the next room. As she pushed the door inwards, she was hit by the smell. She immediately doubled over, dropping her evidence box to the ground, and sprayed vomit all over the back of the door. She cursed and spat the remaining vomit to the floor, wiping her mouth on her sleeve.

Composing herself, she picked her box back up and moved into the room. There was nothing in the room apart from a single bed and an old, brown wooden dressing table. The bed was completely bare, stripped of any bedclothes; which had presumably been taken as evidence. She touched the mattress with her fingertips - it was wet. She raised them to her eye level, and her stomach turned once again when she realised that it was blood. The mattress had been soaked through, from the blood of the victim. She cast her mind back to the photographs that she had inspected of the murder scene. She pictured the poor woman, flesh and muscle exposed as her skin was slowly stripped away. Splatters of blood had collected on the walls around the bed, and some had run down and pooled on the floor.

How could anyone do such a thing? That poor woman must have died in pure agony.

Melissa searched carefully around the bed; she lay down on her side and shone the torch beam beneath it, but found nothing. She pulled away quickly when she noticed that the mattress was seeping, and beginning to drip blood onto the floor below the bed.

Pull yourself together, Melissa, you're a professional.

Walking over to the dressing table, she shone the flashlight around the surface. The beam picked up some deep scratches on the surface, but nothing else. Pulling at the drawer, she attempted to yank it open; it wouldn't budge. She gave it one more hard tug but it stuck fast. As she pulled, she noticed something drop from the back of the table and fall to the floor. She shone the light down and located the item; it had landed underneath the table.

Crouching over, she picked it up and shined the light on it. She held a business card, *The Loft Nightclub – Manchester's Premier Night Spot To Get Sky High*.

Her heartbeat quickened as she turned it over. Printed on the card was the address of the nightclub, and the outline of a fingerprint – in blood.

I cannot believe we missed it. We have a location, if the place had CCTV; we're one-step closer to finding the killer.

She pulled her mobile phone from her pocket to send a text message, but the screen displayed the message – no signal. *Shit.*

Melissa dropped the business card into her pocket, collected her evidence box, and started to make her way towards the door. As she approached the landing, she thought she heard something - a muffled voice. Stopping dead in her tracks, she listened out again, not moving, not breathing.

Everything was silent for a few seconds until she heard it once more, definitely – a muffled voice speaking.

"Help me."

Her pulse rapidly increased, and she thought that her heart was going to thunder out of her chest cavity. Placing down her evidence box quietly, she took two steps forward and carefully peered over the railing and down at the loading bay below. At first, she didn't spot it, but then she noticed that one of the rear doors to the van had been unlocked, and was open. She grabbed her mobile again and checked; still no signal.

Shit.

Melissa dropped her phone back into her pocket and grabbed her pepper spray, slowly clicking the mechanism around to the right, ready for use. Holding the can upright, she placed her thumb on the top of the lid and prepared to point and shoot if required.

As silently as she could, she crept along the landing, listening out for the voice. As she reached the centre, she stopped walking when she heard the voice again, still muffled, but this time a little clearer.

"Help me."

She quickened her pace as she approached the concrete stairway. The van had been parked head on, with the rear door open on the passenger side. She slowly began to descend the flight of stairs, attempting to keep her shoes silent against the concrete steps. When she found herself level with the front of the van, she attempted to peer up over the bonnet to inspect the other side. Looking out around the service yard, she saw nothing, nobody was around, and the whole area was silent. She ducked down at the front of the van and began to edge her way around the front so that she could approach the rear of the van from the driver's side.

With her back to the side of the van, she continued edging herself inch by inch towards the rear of the vehicle. As she reached the last corner, she took a deep breath inwards, then quickly span around to her right, the can held in front of her ready to attack.

There was nobody there.

Inching forward, the can still held aloft ready to attack, Melissa slowly reached the back of the van. Peering into the darkness, she saw nothing. Raising the torch, she clicked on the button to illuminate the vehicle when she saw a dark shadow quickly move and pounce towards her.

Before she could defend herself, her attacker had thrust the blade of a knife directly into her eye socket.

It gave out a sickening cracking sound as the weapon pierced her orb, and blood and liquid sprayed down her cheeks as her attacker pulled the blade back out with a revolting squelching sound.

She shrieked in pain as her left hand immediately went to cover her right eye. Her attacker jumped from the van in front of her, as she tumbled backwards to the concrete on her rump. She held aloft the can of pepper spray and pressed as hard as she could. The stream of chemicals burst out from the can in a fine jet and hit her attacker square in the face; the liquid simply ran down from the leather gimp mask that the attacker was wearing.

The last thing that Melissa remembered before passing out was her attacker producing a soaked cloth in their gloved hand and holding it over her mouth and nose.

Greater Manchester Police Station

DCI Gunn walked back through to the detention sergeant's desk. The man was middle-aged, perhaps fifty years old. His thinning brown hair was receding from his brow, and he had a small moustache that was greying at the edges, and hung unevenly below his top lip. The man was overweight; he clearly enjoyed the diet and lifestyle of the more casual person. His brow was wet with fresh sweat.

Gunn addressed the man.

"Where are you keeping this new guy, Barton? The one who claims to have murdered Gina Hawkins."

"He's in cell number three, sir. Do you want to speak to him?"

"Yes, I want to speak to him before his solicitor arrives."

"But, sir –"

The man never got to finish his sentence as Gunn stormed off towards detention cell number three. Unlocking the door from outside, he stormed into the room.

Sat on the bed was a young man. He was about twenty-five years old, his brown hair was combed over in a messy side parting, and he was slim and gaunt. His face showed the worry lines of a man many years older. He was nervous, and very shifty looking, but Gunn had him summed up in a matter of seconds; *this man is no murderer.*

"I'm DCI Mark Gunn. Tell me everything you know about Chris Daniels."

"Chris Daniels?" The man replied nervously, "I don't know anyone named Chris Daniels."

The detective grabbed the man around the scruff

of his neck and yanked him to his feet, thrusting his forehead into the other man's. He was close enough for him to see the whites of his eyes.

"Don't you fucking lie to me. You know the man. We found a flyer for his business, Daniels Ramsden Partnership, in your dead girlfriend's flat. Explain to me how that got there, if you don't know him."

"I don't know. My girlfriend, she was looking for a property for us to move into together, I'm not sure. I ... I"

Interrupting, he shouted into the man's face, spittle flying from his lips.

"*Shall I tell you what I think, you little shit?* Look at you, you're no fucking murderer, you're barely eight stone dripping wet."

The man didn't respond, he just stared at Gunn with panic and confusion plastered all over his worried face.

"The man that we have in custody is a murderer; he's butchered four women so far, and it was him that killed your girlfriend, Gina Hawkins. We found him at the scene of one of the crimes; somehow, he is getting you to carry the can for it. Is he threatening you? Is that what it is?"

The man didn't respond initially. He stared back at Gunn with a look of pure terror, before suddenly, his face scrunched up in pain, and he suddenly wailed.

"Giiiiiiiiiiiiinnnnnnnnnaaaaaaaaaaaa."

Gunn let the man drop to his knees. His head fell into his hands and he started crying and sobbing desperately.

"Tell me, John. It was Daniels all along, wasn't it?"

The man did not respond, he just rocked back and forth on his knees with his head held in his hands, nodding in pain, wailing and blubbering uncontrollably.

Gunn nodded. "That's good enough for me, kid."

The DCI quickly turned and stormed from the holding cell, and walked back over to the detention sergeant, who continued to stand behind his desk.

"Keep your eye on the kid; he just confessed that he was coerced into a confession by Daniels."

"The other suspect?"

"Yes, I'm going to speak to him now. Let me know when the kid's solicitor arrives. I want to speak to him personally."

"Yes sir, will do."

Gunn stormed down the corridor towards the interrogation room, to Daniels. He stopped for a second, and then turned and headed for the office, where Charlie was sitting intently at her computer screen.

"Charlie."

"Yes, sir?"

"Have you found anything yet?"

"Not yet, I'm just waiting to hear back from the phone company about the sex line on the woman's mobile."

Gunn mused for a moment.

"I've just been to speak to that Barton kid. You can tell from looking at him that he is no murderer. He confessed that Daniels has been threatening him into taking the blame for his girlfriend."

Charlie looked at the detective incredulously.

"He *said* that to you?"

"Yes, and that's why I need you to do something for me."

Charlie looked at him suspiciously.

"What do you need me to do?"

"I need you to shut down the CCTV in the interrogation room so that I can speak to him."

"But, sir..."

"He's our fucking killer, Charlie. The kid has named him, and we found him in the factory at the scene of the crime. How much more convincing do you need?"

"But why do you need me to terminate the camera feed?"

"This guy is a scum-bag. I may need to convince him. It's him, I just know it."

Charlie stared at her boss. She was unsure; she swallowed the nervous lump in her throat. Gunn stared back at her, the look of total harassment etched across his face.

"Okay, I'll re-route the time feed, so that it looks like a glitch with the camera. Please don't tell me that you're going to do anything stupid in there?"

The DCI looked back at Charlie and gave her a sly wink.

"Don't worry; all I need is a few minutes alone time with him. I'll have him singing like a bird."

Charlie watched nervously as Gunn stormed off down the corridor, rolling up the sleeves of his shirt as he walked. She executed the command on her computer screen to disarm the camera in the interrogation room; she had a bad feeling in her gut.

Interrogation room

DCI Gunn stood at the door to the interrogation room, and although it was approaching late afternoon, it was still red hot. His whole body was soaked with a sticky sheen of sweat. His mop of messy, blond hair was soaked through; it clung to his head. His armpits were slippery; you could have wrung out the back of his shirt into a mop bucket.

The adrenaline was rushing through his veins like a stimulant. The man that sat on the opposite side of that door was his killer, and he knew it. He had known it from the second he had laid eyes on him. He took a deep breath and tried to regulate his breathing properly; he had to stay in control of the situation, but enough was enough. He opened the door and entered the room slowly, kicking the door shut behind him. Plaster dust puffed from the wall as it slammed shut in the frame.

Daniels sat quietly in the chair before him. He looked tired and irritable; the day's pressures had started to take its toll in his facial features. Dark shadows had started to form beneath his eyes and his chin and neck had begun to show signs of some early stubble.

He watched Gunn enter the room, and jumped as the door slammed shut behind him. He was sitting at the table; shoulders slumped, with his hands out flat on the surface. The DCI entered the room and sat at the opposite side of the table. He listlessly ran his fingers through his hair and blew the air out from between his lips.

The man spoke first. "DCI Gunn, I've now been in your custody for hours. You haven't told me whether or not I need to speak to my solicitor, and quite frankly, I'm getting a little fed up."

The DCI did not initially respond. He stared at the man; his eyes bore into him before replying impassively. "Why did you kill Gina Hawkins?"

"What? I don't even know a Gina Hawkins."

Gunn sighed. "What about a John Barton?"

"I don't know a John Barton either. What's this all about?"

Gunn laughed. "Well, if that's the way that you're going to play it. Let us look at the evidence that we have, shall we. You're a suspect in connection with the murder of four women. We find you at the crime scene of the last victim. You're a known rapist that got off on a technicality, and the real cherry on the cake is that I have a young guy down in the hall in custody that has named you for coercing him to take the blame for murdering his girlfriend."

Daniel looked at Gunn, his eyes narrowed. He swallowed down a lump in his throat, and he shook his head slightly, in disbelief.

"I don't know what game you are trying to play here, *detective*, but I'm not saying another goddamn word until I've seen my solicitor."

Gunn stared at the man; the veins in his temples began to throb under the pressure.

"Just confess to it Daniels; you killed those women didn't you? You piece of shit."

"I've told you, Gunn, I'm not saying another goddamn word until I've seen my solicitor."

Something inside Gunn's mind snapped. He leapt up from his chair and grabbed Daniels by his mop of hair. The man winced in pain and grabbed at his hands, trying to alleviate the pressure as Gunn started to pull him upwards from his chair.

"You did it, didn't you? You killed those girls."

The man didn't respond, he attempted to wrap his fingers around Gunn's, in a futile attempt to relieve his grip.

Gunn spat, "You killed them, didn't you?"

Again, the man gave no response; he simply grunted in pain.

Gunn then slammed the man's head down onto the table. His face cracked against the hard surface, smashing cartilage and bone. He pulled the man's head back upright. A sliver of blood ran from his nose, dripping down his chin. Both of his eyes had already started to blacken.

He shouted again. "*Confess, you did it didn't you?*"

The man didn't respond.

Gunn reciprocated the suspect's silence by slamming his face down into the desk once again, even harder than the last. Then he did it again, and again. By the time he'd pulled the man's head back upright, he was unconscious – out cold.

"You're a real piece of shit," he spat, and let go of the man's hair. He fell back into the seat and slumped sideways as he was unable to maintain his own sense of balance. He fell to the floor of the interrogation room with a loud thump, the side of his face hitting the tiled floor with a wet slap.

The door to the interrogation room suddenly swung open as Gunn stood over the unconscious man, his face dripping with sweat, his breathing laboured from exertion. Charlie and the detention sergeant looked at him. A complete look of horror spread across their faces. The sergeant's mouth dropped open in disbelief when he saw the man, blood beginning to form beneath his head on the floor.

Charlie was the first to speak. "Sir, my God, what have you done?"

Gunn snapped round to face the other two police officers, a wild, feral look emanating from his face. "I did what I had to do," he spat. "I got a confession."

He then stormed back towards the doorway, the desk sergeant sidestepped out of his way, avoiding his charge. Charlie didn't move in time and caught the full brunt of his shoulder in her chest, winding her, sending her reeling sideways. She fell to the floor on her rump, wincing in pain.

Gunn shouted over his shoulder.

"Call that bastard an ambulance, and ensure that someone is sent up to the hospital to guard him. I'm going up to see the Chief Constable."

Manchester – Unknown location.

Melissa stirred, her head feeling heavy and sore. She opened her eyes as an excruciating pain shot down the side of her face. She could see nothing but a bright white light. Closing her eyes for a moment to try to ease the pain, she realised that her arms were tightly bound. Panic overcame her; she opened her eyes again, ignoring the agony, trying to see where she was, but still she could see nothing but blazing white. Gritting her teeth in an attempt to block out the shooting pain that was taking over the right side of her face, she lifted her arms, struggling to free them. The binds were too tight; even without her vision, she knew that they hadn't moved at all. She could feel it.

Opening her mouth, Melissa tried to scream for help, but nothing happened. It was like the fear had possessed her vocal chords. She strained, but nothing other than a gentle wheeze escaped from her lips.

Sat in silence, any signs of optimism began to fade away.

She knew that there was no hope. She was tied up, couldn't see, and couldn't shout for help. She thought about giving up, going to sleep, in the hope that it would soon be over. Hot tears begin to drip from the corner of her eye, it stung and burned.

"*Ahhhhhh!*" Finally, the scream escaped, but what followed was nothing but sheer silence.

"Please, someone help me," Melissa whimpered.

She heard something to her side. In reflex, she turned to see who or what was there, then realised that she still couldn't see anything. Sitting still once again, hoping she was facing forwards, she tried to focus on listening for that sound again, finding it difficult to concentrate because of the pain. She sat perfectly still.

Breathing. She could hear someone breathing right next to her. While she sat and focused for a moment, she could actually feel the warmth of their breath on the side of her face.

"Oh my God!" she screamed. "Who are you? What do you want? Please, *let me go*."

No one answered.

The breathing continued. Melissa screamed once again, and then she heard footsteps moving from beside her, circling her until they were behind her.

Someone ripped the blindfold from her head. A piercing light sent shockwaves of pain through her entire body. After a second, the light dimmed a little, and she was able to see, but only out of one eye. That's when she remembered, before she passed out. Someone stabbed her in the eye. That's why she felt all this pain. Her goddamn eye was gone.

A shuffling noise came from beside her; she turned quickly to see a blurred shadow. She couldn't make out who it was, just a silhouette with something shining beside them. In a blurred motion, the glimmering object moved swiftly toward her face. A second later, darkness and pain followed. Melissa could feel the blood pouring from her face like a fountain. She screamed in agony, streams of a mixture of blood, tears and sticky substances seeped from the two remaining holes in her face.

"*Why?*" she screamed.

No reply. Once again, she sat with nothing but silence. Her head began to feel heavy and started to sag. She knew that, at any minute, she was going to pass out. The pain now was just too much to deal with. Her head felt as though it was being kicked from every direction. Ringing filled her ears, she couldn't even hear her own sobbing anymore.

A lifetime seemed to pass when suddenly; Melissa heard footsteps in the room once more. She didn't know whether she had passed out or not. The pain was still there, but seemed to have subsided by an enormous amount. Her guess was that she had been unconscious for a while. If she didn't know any better, she would have guessed that she had been given some pain medication.

"Listen, I don't know anything. I can't even see anything now. You know I can't identify you. Please, just let me go."

A bolt of lightning agony shot from Melissa's wrist, and up her arm. Instinctively, she drew her hand to her mouth to brace the pain. Something wet slapped her in the face, and she only had a second to realise that she was only able to move her arm because the bind was gone, and so was her hand. Suddenly, her useless arm was pinned back down and a red-hot pain scorched her, searing what she now knew was her bloody stump. She could smell her own skin melting and cauterising.

Darkness began to fill her mind, her head sagged once more and slowly, she began to pass out. Just before consciousness departed completely, her head was pushed back against the chair for a moment, and she heard a noise.

The shutter of a camera.

Chief Constable's Office.

The room was filled with the sound of a fluttering keyboard, the squeak of a leather chair, and the frustrated grunts of Chief Constable Rollins. The recent news coverage of this murder spree was beginning to take its toll on him. News reporters followed him from the office to his home, with never ending questions, hot on his tail, wherever he went.

This problem felt like it was going to be getting a lot worse before it improved.

Perspiration began to pool on his forehead. If he carried on letting this get to him as much as it was, then he knew he was going to lose his wife. She'd already told him that she couldn't cope with his mood swings, the aggression, the erratic behaviour. The last time they had a case this big; it led to his wife leaving him for almost a month. He wasn't sure if he would be able to cope with that again, not this time.

He was older now, wiser - he needed her.

A quick knock on the door alerted Rollins, and before he could summon the person, DCI Gunn burst into the room. He was red faced, looking like he'd just been on a run, or in a fight, which wasn't unusual for him. His reputation hadn't gotten lost on its way to the Chief Constable's office. It wasn't something Rollins would ever admit in public, but the way Gunn handled things was something that he greatly admired. Not enough officers like that nowadays. The world had gone crazy with too much political correctness.

Well, sometimes aggression saved lives, and Gunn had saved more than a few.

"So how can I help you, Mr Gunn?" Rollins leaned back in his chair.

"I've got him." A grin spread across Gunn's bright red face.

Rollins sat forward, leaning on his desk. Trying not to appear too excited.

"What do you mean, you've got him?"

"Well, I've got a confession from Daniels, and a statement from Barton saying that Daniels threatened him to take the blame."

Finally, this was it, they could put all of this behind them. As soon as everything was finalised, Rollins would get Gunn to issue a press release and those goddamn reporters would leave him alone. He would actually be able to get a good night's sleep.

"Okay," Rollins said. "Run me through exactly what they've said. Is this nailed on? Are we sure we've got the right guy here?"

"Chief, you don't confess to murder if you're not the guy who did it." Gunn exclaimed. "Well, unless you're being threatened to, of course. I went to question Barton about his confession. I knew from one look at him that he wasn't the killer. You know what it's like, Chief. When you've been in the game as long as we have, you can spot a killer from a mile away."

"True. Go on", Rollins replied.

"Well, after looking at him and guessing he wasn't the killer, I had a little word. I asked him what was going on, why he was doing this. You know, the usual drill. That's when he told me that Daniels had been threatening him into a confession."

"Okay, so what happened then? How did this lead to the confession from Daniels?"

"Well, of course, after Barton had told me that, I went straight to see Daniels, and asked him about it. I told him that Barton had fingered him for the crime and that we knew he'd been threatening Barton to take the blame. After I had a little talk, he confessed to everything."

Rollins raised an eyebrow. He knew exactly what Gunn's "little talks" consisted of. If this was a confession that had been beaten out of the guy, then it might not necessarily be true.

"So, what exactly did this little talk go like?" he asked.

Gunn smiled.

"Well you know what it's like, Chief. A game of chess, my move, his move, back and forth and all that."

"Right, okay. Let me have a look at the statements to be sure we're covered. Have you got them with you now?"

Gunn turned as though he was walking out of the door, and then stopped for a moment. He scratched the back of his head and then turned back to face the Chief. His face had reddened more now. Rollins couldn't tell whether it was embarrassment or anger. He knew what was coming next.

"The thing is, Chief," Gunn said, "about the statements."

"Please don't tell me that you've come in here talking of confessions without any signed statements to back them up." Rollins face was tight lipped and furious.

"I'll get the statements signed, it was an in the moment thing. You know how it is sometimes. You get them talking and before you know it, they've said everything you need before you get a chance to write anything down."

Rollins rolled his eyes. This was a fine line of bullshit, if he'd ever heard one.

"Forget it, you can sort the statements at a later date then. Go and get me the CCTV footage. That has sound so it can act as a statement in itself. They use them in the States all the time."

Gunn's face transformed from the big hard man that everyone at the station was used to seeing, into something which resembled a little boy being chastised by an angry head teacher.

"Well, Chief. I umm..."

"You what?" Rollins asked sternly. "Just go and get me the footage."

"I had them turn the cameras off before I entered the rooms."

"You've got to be *kidding* me." Rollins jaw dropped.

"It was the only way I was getting a confession from this guy."

"So you kicked the shit out of him?"

"Not to that extent," Gunn answered. "I may have given him a little slap. Or two."

"*For God's sake, Gunn!*" Rollins roared. "So you come in here telling me you've got no written statements, no CCTV footage, just a confession that you beat out of our only real suspect. When the press gets hold of this they're going to have a fucking field day."

"They won't get hold of it. This is the guy, Chief. I'm sure of..."

"It doesn't matter what you think you are *sure of*," Rollins interrupted. "You know how this works. We need evidence or a *signed* confession. What you have isn't worth shit."

"I'll get it."

"You best had, or I wouldn't bother coming back into work tomorrow. If you've left any marks on that man, there is nothing I can do to protect you."

"I'll get the confession," Gunn said through gritted teeth.

"Well get it, and get it fucking right this time. Now go!" Rollins slammed both fists on his desk.

Gunn left the room, slamming the door on his way out. The silence in Rollins' office shattered with the noise of his teeth grinding together. This was definitely getting a lot worse before it got better.

Greater Manchester Police Station

Jessica climbed out of her car and broke into a sprint to enter the doors to the station. Looking flushed and slightly out of breath, she leaned on the reception desk.

"Where's DCI Gunn?"

"Last I saw he was going to see the Chief Constable."

"Okay, thanks."

Jessica marched along the hallway and up the stairs toward the Chief Constable's office. When she reached the top of the stairs, she attempted to open the door, but before she managed to pull it, the door flew wide open knocking her backwards a few steps. She almost lost her balance and fell down the stairs before someone grabbed her shoulders, and pulled her back up, helping Jessica regain her balance.

After composing herself she looked to see that her rescuer, and almost killer, was DCI Gunn.

"Watch where you're going," Gunn spat.

"*Me?*" Jessica shouted in a high-pitched voice. "Why don't you watch where *you're* going? You almost knocked me down the stairs."

"Yeah, well, I caught you didn't I? Always be prepared for a door to open." Gunn gave her a sarcastic grin and then jogged past her, down the stairs.

"Wait." Jessica turned and followed. "I need to talk to you."

Gunn was speeding away with long strides, Jessica had to jog to catch up and then stay alongside him.

"Will you hold on for a minute?" She panted.

"I can't, I've got to go and get this bastard to sign a confession."

"That's what I want to talk to you about. I don't

know how you got him to confess but…"

"*Don't you start as well*," Gunn yelled, making the other officers in the corridor stop and stare. "I know that this is the guy. I just need him to sign the document."

"But it can't be."

"What the hell do you mean it can't be? I know it is."

"But I…" Jessica stuttered.

"What happened to your face?" Gunn asked. His mood suddenly changed from that of an angry bear, to something that now resembled a caring father or older brother. Jessica could see in his eyes that he genuinely cared.

"I, umm…" Tears began to pool in Jessica's eyes.

Gunn put his arm around her and led her into the staff room. He walked to the small kitchen compartment and poured a cup of coffee. He passed it to her as she took a seat. It was black, she usually added milk, but right now, she didn't question it. She just sipped from the cup.

"Listen, I'm sorry about before. I was just a bit stressed," Gunn said. "This case is really getting to me, you know?"

"Yeah, I know. It's getting to us all," Jessica said, then took another sip.

"Right, so now we've calmed down a bit. Do you want to tell me what happened to your face?"

Jessica burst into tears. She tried to talk, but kept hyperventilating. Gunn moved forward and grabbed her, pulling her close into what felt like a bear hug. His big arms wrapped all the way around her, almost like he could hug her twice over. She had never felt so safe in anyone's arms before. She composed herself and looked up into his eyes.

"I lost him," She whispered.

"Lost who?"

"The killer."

"You couldn't have. I told you, I've got him in the…"

"No, you've got the wrong guy." She stepped back and Gunn let go of her.

"I'm confident this is the guy."

"*No!*" Jessica shouted. Gunn looked shocked. "You haven't got the right guy. The right guy did this to me."

A look of terror washed over Gunn's face.

"He got you? Did you see him? How did you get away?"

Jessica shook her head as though disapproving herself. "I was back at the crime scene looking for some more evidence, anything that might be helpful. I found a pair of police issue cuffs, and a blonde hair. Before I knew it, this guy rushed me and punched me in the face. I didn't get a chance to look at him."

"Well, how do you know it was our killer? People can buy those handcuffs anywhere, it could have been anyone." Gunn exclaimed.

"Do you really believe that?"

"Shit." Gunn looked to the ceiling and let out a sigh. "I've fucked up."

"The killer is still out there somewhere, we just…"

Jessica was interrupted by the sound of a text message to her phone. She grabbed it from her pocket. "It's Melissa."

"What does it say?" Gunn asked.

"Hang on, it's a picture, it's taking a second to come through."

Gunn walked to Jessica's side so he too could look at the phone. Jessica held it out further so they both had a clear view. Then the picture came through.

"Oh, my…" Jessica dropped her phone. Gunn quickly scooped down to collect it.

The picture delivered to the phone was of Melissa, her face washed red with blood, two dark red holes where her eyes used to be.

"*Fuck!*" Gunn spat and punched the wall, leaving a hole behind. "I swear to God, I will find this bastard, and I'm going to kill him."

Killer's Got His Gunn

Trying to keep up with the pace, I wanted to make sure that she didn't leave my sight. Rain splashed on my boots, and soaked through to my socks. Glancing to a road sign, I noticed the street name: Cooper Street.

Where's she going?

Seeing the woman take a turn, she followed a flight of stairs down into a basement bar. I held back for a moment, pausing. It would be a bad idea to get half way down the stairs, and then have to turn around again straight away because she decided to backtrack.

After a minute or so, it seemed that she was staying in the bar. Entering the dimly lit room, I walked across the room and ordered a single Jack Daniels, on ice. Glancing around, I could see that the bar was empty apart from myself. It couldn't be that she had snuck out without me noticing, could it?

I address the barman, a tall, gangly fellow. "Hey … It's pretty quiet isn't it? Am I the only one here?"

The barman smiled. "It's the middle of the day; it's always quiet at this time."

"Yeah, but you'd think *someone* else would be here."

"Nope, just you."

He turned around and began drying the glass in his hand. I begin to worry.

"Oh, and her. The girl who came in soaking wet."

Turning around nonchalantly, I see the woman returning from the toilet.

"Ah I see."

The barman nodded. "Now you can have some company while you drink."

"Not right now. I prefer my own company. Until I'm a few drinks in, at least."

"Suit yourself."

Seeing the woman go to one end of the bar, I keep a watchful eye. I edged towards the other end, but kept just close enough to hear any conversation or comments.

In an Irish accent, I hear her place her drink order. "I'll have a Corona, please."

It's definitely her, it can't be a coincidence.

Sitting patiently and sipping my drink, I watch her swaying back and forth while listening to the band practicing on the other side of the room. Before long, she utters something to the barman about it ordering another drink.

My cue.

This was the moment. No time like the present.

I approached cautiously and then leaned into her.

"Let me get that for you."

Tiger Lounge – Manchester

Charlie marched along Cooper Street, puddles splashing beneath her with each step. The rain was harsh and cold, it fitted well with her mood. When she reached The Tiger Lounge, her hair was dripping wet. She walked through the door and took her coat off. It was a basement bar, so she had to make her way down the stairs. Water dripped from her coat as she made her way down, leaving a trail behind her.

When she arrived at the bar, she stood for a moment waiting to catch the barman's attention. Crouched down, he was filling the fridge with bottles of lager. A pool of water began to form around Charlie as it still dripped from her hair.

"Hello," Charlie finally called.

"Sorry, didn't see you there," the barman said, while rising to his feet.

"Do you have a towel or something I could use? I'm dripping wet here."

"I've only got bar towels here, and trust me you don't want to use one of them. Best bet is the hand dryer in the bathroom. It's just over there." He gestured to the back of the room.

"Okay, thank you."

A few minutes later, Charlie returned from the bathroom, now a little drier. Her hair still sat flat on her face from the rain, but at least it wasn't dripping anymore. She retrieved her phone from her pocket, checking it worked, ensuring the rain hadn't broken it. After a quick glance at the black screen, she remembered that she had turned her phone off. Having been furious with DCI Gunn's actions earlier that day, she'd decided that she didn't want to be contacted by him, or anyone else today. She just wanted to sit and have a drink, and forget about everything for a little while.

"So what'll it be?" The barman smiled.

"I'll have a Corona, please."

"Glass?"

"No, just in the bottle with a slice of lime, thanks."

"Irish? I thought you lot preferred the stronger stuff."

"Oh, don't you worry. I'm pretty sure the stronger stuff will be following soon enough." Charlie sighed and took a gulp out of her bottle.

"One of those days, eh?"

"You have no idea."

A band was playing on the stage behind her. *"Turn on the TV it attacks your mind; just wanna put up your feet."*

"Hey," Charlie said to the bar man. "These are pretty good, who are they?"

"Local band, Lovechild. Yeah, people seem to like them."

Charlie looked around at the nearly empty bar. "There's not a lot of people here right now?"

"That's because it's only four o' clock, and they're just practising." The bar man laughed. "You're starting early. Can I get you another?"

"Yeah, sure. Be rude not to, wouldn't it?" Charlie smiled.

She turned back to watch the band for a while. It felt good to be away from all the stress and drama of the past couple of days. Turning her phone off was the best thing she could have done. It gave her a complete escape. Well, almost a complete escape. Even now, her brain was working overtime, trying to piece things together. They had to be missing something - she just knew it.

She was sure that Daniels wasn't the killer. She was also sure that the truth would come out about how Gunn made him confess, and that was going to do nothing other than make solving this case more difficult. She knew Gunn was a good cop, but sometimes he just lost it; let the case overwhelm him, the risk of him throwing it all away by turning into a mindless thug was a constant. As police officers, they were meant to be better than that. Plus, the way he barged past her and knocked her to the ground, without even glancing back to see if she was okay.

Goddammit, he made her so angry.

She shook her head and drained the rest of her bottle.

"Hey, can I get another?"

"Let me get that for you." A smiling face appeared next to Charlie.

"Oh …Hello," Charlie smiled. "Do I know you?"

"Not yet, but you will."

Charlie laughed. "Oh, *really*?"

The barman put another drink in front of them, which Charlie happily collected. She quickly drained that one as well. "I tell you what." Charlie said. "I think it's time for the stronger stuff. How about a little bourbon for me and my new *friend* here."

The bar man raised an eyebrow, and glanced at Charlie. It was obvious she was already getting pretty drunk. He looked to the new arrival. "Bourbon?"

"Sure, why not. Let's make them doubles."

DCI Gunn stood outside the front of the police station, the cigarette placed between his lips. A squeal of tyres welcomed a new arrival, and Gunn saw a sporty red BMW pulling to the kerb. Jessica sat in the passenger seat, and he noticed Alex, Jessica's partner, sitting in the driver's seat. Gunn rolled his eyes as the pair engaged in a passionate kiss. The car door opened and Jess hopped out of the vehicle before it sped away, the horn papping.

Jessica addressed Gunn. "Morning, sir."

"What kept you? We have work to do."

Everyone in the station was avoiding the proverbial storm that was DCI Gunn, as he marched around the station with a purpose. His aggression over the last few days had been excessive, even for him. Now, with the recent news of Melissa Lason, no one wanted to be the one to piss him off, or worse, push him over the edge.

Barging the staff room door open, people scurried out of the way like ants. Within a minute, only one person other than Gunn was left in the room; Jessica, who'd walked beside him. She glanced at her superior, and gave a half-hearted smile.

"So…"

Gunn nodded. "How you doin'? You sleep okay?"

"No, not really. I kept seeing Melissa's face, it won't disappear. I just can't believe that it's happened to her. I never thought *we* were at risk."

"Of course we are. If anything, we're more at risk than others. We're closer to this than anyone else."

"Yeah, I understand that. I mean, getting

attacked by a killer who's trying to escape is one thing. We're ready for that, but the picture he sent of Melissa?" Jessica sighed. "That looked like he really put a lot of effort into it. Like he really enjoyed it.

Gunn could see Jessica's eyes pooling with tears. He could feel a knot turning in his stomach as well. He needed to change the subject quickly, before they both became a blubbering mess, and he certainly wasn't going to let anyone at the station see weakness coming from him.

"Where's Charlie?" he asked. "It's not like her to be late."

"I haven't seen her yet. Perhaps she's just a bit slow this morning. It's getting to all of us. Maybe the news of Melissa was a bit too much for her."

"I haven't told her about Melissa yet, have you?" Gunn asked.

"No, I didn't speak to anyone after that yesterday. I just went home to sleep, well, try to. I thought you called her? You said you were going to call her when I was leaving."

"Yes, I did. Well, I mean, I tried. I called her a few times, but her phone was turned off."

Jessica's face turned white. "You don't think…"

"No, no," Gunn said. "I'm sure she'll be fine. She was a bit pissed off with me yesterday, and rightly so. I barged her out of the way and knocked her down. I was so angry at the time that I didn't even turn back to help her."

"Why?" Jessica looked shocked.

"It wasn't intentional. She was just in the way at the time. You saw the way I was yesterday. I don't mean to be like that, but sometimes it just takes control of me. We're all struggling here, I'm no different."

"Yeah, I know what you mean. Well, why don't you give her a call now? We really need to let her know."

Gunn took his phone out of his pocket and called Charlie. It went straight to voicemail. He moved the phone away from his ear and looked at Jessica.

She nodded. "I have a really bad feeling about this."

"Me too. Come on, we'll go to her place now. I'm sure she's fine," he reassured, "but it's better to be safe than sorry, isn't it?"

On the way out of the station, Gunn told his other colleagues where they were going, and that if Charlie showed up, she had to call him straight away. He jumped into his car, with Jessica close behind. He revved the engine and then steered out of the car park.

Jessica felt sick as Gunn threw the car around each corner.

"Can't you slow down a little bit?" she said.

"This isn't even fast," Gunn laughed. "Watch this."

He accelerated more, laughing as he could see Jessica's fingers gripping deep into the side of her chair. He skidded around another corner and then suddenly came to an abrupt stop.

"We're here." He smiled.

Jessica, grey faced and shaken, jumped out of the car. She stood still for a moment, leaning slightly, holding onto her stomach.

"You okay?" Gunn laughed. "Not gonna be sick are you?"

"Do you always drive like that?" Jessica asked.

"Sure, I just like to get from A to B as quickly as my wheels will take me. What's the point in fast cars if you're not gonna use them? Plus, it's good practice. Never know when I'm going to have a high speed chase, do I?"

"Sure, whatever." Jessica shook her head and walked toward Charlie's front door.

Standing side by side, they knocked on the door

and waited. After a moment, when there was no answer, Gunn knocked again, this time a lot louder. Still no answer. Now he was banging on the door with the side of a clenched fist.

"*Charlie!*" he shouted. "Are you in there? Are you okay?"

"I'll try her phone again." Jessica said, and dialled the number. After a moment, she hung up. "Nope, it's still going to answerphone."

Gunn tried to look through the window, but the curtains were closed. He couldn't see a thing. He banged on the door again.

"Should I go and check around the back?" Jessica asked.

Gunn took a deep breath and stared at the door. "You know what?" he said. "Fuck it, I'll pay her back."

He lunged at the door and flung his size twelve boot accurately at the lock. The door splintered and flew open. Jessica stood staring at him, her mouth wide open.

"Ladies first," he said, smiling.

Tentatively, they both stepped into the house. It was dark and smelled strongly of alcohol. They crept forward slowly, both waiting in anticipation for someone to jump out at any minute. Gunn moved to the window and swiftly pulled the curtains apart.

"*Shit!*" Jessica screamed from behind him.

Gunn quickly turned ready to attack the source of her fright. When he saw the sight in front of him, his legs almost buckled. Lying on her back with her arms and legs side by side, was Charlie. She was a grey, bluish colour. It wouldn't take a mortician to tell them that she was dead. Her jaw was forced wide, hinged open with something shoved inside of it, leaving her mouth in an eternal scream.

"What the hell is that?" Gunn asked, while reaching for the object.

"*You can't touch it,*" Jessica quickly shouted.

Gunn looked at her.

"It's evidence."

"She's not just some dead body," *Gunn* said. "She's part of my team. *Our* team."

He reached for the object and pulled it from her mouth. It was a camera. He looked to Jessica fearfully. There was a play button on the side of the device. After a deep breath, he pressed the button.

"Jessica. There's still footage on this camera."

****

Gunn held the small digital device in the palm of his hand. He and Jessica watched the grainy pixels begin to form a picture. At first, it was difficult to make out anything on the screen, as the picture was mostly dark and covered with shadows. They both stared intently as the camera slowly panned backwards, widening the shot. Both officers did a double take at the realisation of what they were viewing.

Bound to a steel chair by her arms, with thick, black leather straps, sat Melissa, still wearing the same clothes that she had been wearing the last time that they had seen her. Her black hair was slick with sweat and was stuck down to her forehead and cheeks. Two gaping, bloody holes were now where her eyes once sat. Streams of dark blood, tears and sweat had dried on her face.

Jess put her hand up to her mouth, resisting the urge to vomit. Gunn turned the camera to its side, frantically searching for the audio controls.

"Where is the fucking volume on this thing?"

Locating the small button on the side of the camera, he held it down until the audible crackling came through the speakers. A faint hissing sound, and then a voice spoke from off the camera. It sounded odd, altered in some way, as if it had some kind of electrical tinge to it.

"Speak."

"What… what do you want me to say?" Melissa asked.

Suddenly, a gloved hand appeared on the screen and the index finger of the hand ran down Melissa's cheek. The woman flinched at the touch of the finger as it continued to trace itself down her face. The sound of a blood-curdling scream echoed around the room, and Jessica doubled over and threw up as the finger of the hand pushed itself into the hole in the woman's face, where her eye once was; a reddish and brown liquid squirted out as the finger continued to rummage around in the socket, before pulling out. Melissa continued to scream and thrash her head about in pain.

Setting his jaw, Gunn continued to watch. The same voice came on to the camera again. "Melissa, we talked about what I wanted you to say to your colleagues. If you continue to be worthless, I will dispose of you now."

Melissa stopped screaming and gritted her teeth, beginning to take in heavy breaths of air, struggling to keep her body from buckling.

From the gaping apertures in her face, where her beautiful eyes once sat, she faced the camera, a fresh torrent of gore streaming down her face, and dripping from her chin, onto her clothing.

She stuttered. "In Charlie's breast pocket, there is a note."

"And?" The voice replied.

"It's for your eyes only, Gunn."

DCI Gunn looked at Jessica, a look of deep concern spreading across both of their faces, before the voice on camera spoke again.

"DCI Gunn, you have a choice. You are in control of whether Melissa here lives or dies. Everything is explained in the letter."

The picture on the screen faded, replaced with a

white fuzz. Gunn looked at Jessica. "What do you think?"

"I don't like the sound of it, sir."

"Neither do I, but it looks like we don't have much of a choice. Here, hold this."

He passed the camera to Jessica, who held it between her fingertips.

"We should get this dusted for fingerprints, sir."

"First thing's first," he replied, turning to look at the cold, dead body of his former colleague. He knelt beside her corpse and carefully began to examine the woman's clothing. Frisking down the arms and inside of her jacket, he found nothing apart from a small mirror. Continuing to search, he searched through the side pockets of her trousers until his fingers located something. He pulled the item from her pocket. Jessica continued to watch as Gunn opened up the note and began to read.

As he inspected the rough handwriting on the page, it seemed inconsistent and erratic, as if were rushed or perhaps written by someone using their non-dominant hand. He began to read the note, and his heart rate quickened. He swallowed the massive lump that appeared in his throat. He finished reading the instructions on the page, and then began to read them once more from the beginning. When he was finished, he looked at Jessica. She could tell from the look on his face that it was not good news.

"What did the note say, sir?"

He didn't respond, he stared at her, without saying a word.

Jessica spoke again, snapping the officer from his reverie. "Sir, can I see the note?"

"I have to go," he replied.

"What do you mean, sir? The note. What did it say?"

Completely ignoring the question, he folded the note back up and placed it into his trouser pocket. He turned and took another glance at his fallen colleague, before turning back to Jessica.

"I have to go," he began, "there is only one way that I can save us all."

"What do you mean, sir? Please, what did the note say?"

Gunn turned and began to quickly stride towards the door. Jessica stood between him and the entrance and screamed. "*Sir, I can't let you go anywhere until I know what was in that letter.*"

Gunn stopped moving forward, and stood a few feet away from Jessica as she covered the door. "Move out of my way, Jess, I don't want you to get hurt."

Jessica pulled the can of pepper spray from her inside pocket and held it up to Gunn's face. She shouted. "Sir, I need you to tell me what you know, now."

Gunn spat. "Get that fucking thing out of my face, now, before I break your arm."

Jessica continued to hold the can at an arm's length, ready to spray at any moment.

"I'm going to give you to the count of three. Put the can down, Jess."

"Please, sir, just –"

"One." He began.

Jessica's hand began to shake as she held out the can, her finger held down on the nozzle, ready to spray.

"Two."

Jessica looked into Gunn's eyes; he had a look of sheer determination upon his face, his eyes were bulging and his teeth gritted. He took a small step towards her.

"Three."

Before he could react, Jessica held down the nozzle on the can, spraying the chemicals from the can, directly into the man's face. He screamed as the spray went to work, pain igniting his face in agony as the liquid attacked and burned his nerve endings. Still wincing in pain, he lunged forwards and grabbed the can from Jessica, throwing it to one side, the can bouncing up from the carpeted floor and rolling off across the room.

One hand gripped around her wrist, he grabbed her shoulder with his left hand, using his strength and momentum, and he launched the woman across the room. Staggering forwards, she was unable to stop herself from falling to the side as her forehead connected with the wall. Her skull bounced off the plasterboard, leaving a head shaped dent in the wall, plumes of plaster dust bounced from the hole as she fell to the side. She was out cold before she landed on the floor.

Gunn frantically wiped at his face with his sleeve, attempting to clear the spray from his eyes. He clumsily ran into the kitchen, bouncing into doorframes and work surfaces as he clambered his way frantically to the sink.

Clawing at the tap, in desperation, he turned on the cold water as quickly as the stream would flow. He splashed the water all over his face greedily, washing the chemicals from his skin. Repeating the process another few times, he quickly moved back into the living room, and kneeled down besides Jessica. He placed his two fingers on the side of her neck, checking for her pulse.

"I'm sorry that it had to be this way, kid. In the long run, you will understand."

He rolled her over so that she was face down on the carpet and placed her into the recovery position. Standing, he took one last look around, and then turned. Running from the house, he slammed the door behind him and made his way to his car.

Unlocking the key with the fob, he jumped into the driving seat and quickly started the engine. He checked his reflection in the rear view mirror, his eyes were blood shot and tears continued to stream down his face from the pepper spray. The skin around his eyes and cheeks were blood red. Slamming the car into gear, he pulled away, wheels spinning.

The sun was beginning to shine brightly, there was not a single cloud in the sky as Gunn steered his car through the busy city centre traffic. He checked the clock on his car dashboard, and it read 10:40 a.m. We wiped the sweat from his brow with the back of his sleeve. As he sped in and out of the lanes, narrowly avoiding collision after collision, he thought back to the note that he had recovered from Charlie's body:

Detective Constable Gunn, as you can see from my body count, I am not messing about. One member of your team is already dead, and another I have in my clutches. It is up to you whether she dies, as is the same for the last member of your team, Jessica. The blood of every one of my victim's is on your hands.

The officer racked his brains trying to think who could be behind it all. His somewhat unorthodox methods over the years had led to him making a whole number of enemies.

If you want the remaining members of your team to live, you need to meet with me. All will become clear. Ensure that you come alone. Ensure that you are unarmed. If I get any predisposition that you have not followed these instructions; the remaining members of your team will be subjected to a slow and painful death.

Gunn slowed slightly as he grabbed the note from his trouser pocket. Clumsily, he opened the letter, continuing to steer the car at speed with his knees up against the underside of the steering wheel. Checking once more, he threw the car around the next right hand turn, and continued to speed in the direction of the district of Prestwick, located in the north-western region of the city.

Come to the address shown below. Again, I remind you to ensure that you come alone. You know that there are further lives at stake. At the location, you will drive onto an industrial estate, where there is an unused unit; Number 37, isolated at the rear of the estate. There is an old sign displayed 'Car Body Panels and Lamps.' To the side of the factory unit, there is a damaged steel fence. Duck through the gap and enter into the premises by a blue personnel door towards the rear of the building.

Looking up from the note, he didn't spot the car until the last second.

He swung the steering wheel around sharply to the left, but couldn't avoid the collision as his car hit the other vehicle side on, at speed. There was a massive thumping and scraping of metal against metal as Gunn's car slammed into the passenger door, spinning the other car around quickly, showering the road and footpath in broken glass. With the steering wheel locked around, as he attempted to avoid the collision, his car tipped over violently onto its side and began to slide, before coming to an abrupt stop a few seconds later.

The eruption of pain in his leg was immediate, as the metal crumpled beneath him and trapped his leg in place; the airbag went off inches from his face.

Gunn lay still for a few moments, his world spinning. His chest erupted into agony from where he had struck the steering wheel. He sensed the sour, coppery scent of blood as it coated the back of his throat; he coughed up blood into his hand.

You're hurt, bad. Probably a crushed lung.

Unfastening his seat belt, he attempted to twist around and pull himself free from the seat, screaming in agony as he attempted to pull his twisted ankle from its trap within the crumpled metal. Stopping for a second to gain composure, he attempted to take a deep breath inwards, which resulted in another coughing fit. Somehow managing to twist himself upwards, his prime consideration was getting out of the vehicle in case it caught fire. Dragging his damaged, bloody leg below him, he pushed upwards and attempted to push open the door. Due to its own weight, it would not budge, no matter how hard he shoved. He attempted to push upwards with his shoulder but the door would not move due to its own weight.

Realising that the engine was still running, he pushed the window release button with his thumb. At first, nothing happened. He repeated the process until the glass suddenly started to whirr downwards, opening an escape hatch. Locking the underside of his elbows onto the doorframe, he pulled himself upwards, his shoulders straining as he attempted to lift his own body weight. Jamming the knee of his good leg into the intersection of the car door, he pulled himself free.

He screamed out in agony as his leg hit the concrete and a blast of pain shot up from his ankle, through his entire body, and into his skull. Rolling onto his back, he stared up at the blue sky. The sun shone down on his face; a thick film of perspiration began to appear due to the heat.

A voice spoke from a man who stood above him, his shadow covering Gunn's face from the sun's glare.

"Hey, man, are you alright? I've phoned for an ambulance."

With all of the strength that he could muster, he sat himself upwards and stared at the man. He was a young man in his early twenties with long brown hair, tied back into a ponytail. He wore Bermuda shorts and sandals.

"What about the other car?" he asked.

"Shit, man, she doesn't look so hot."

Slowly, with the aid of the man, Gunn pulled himself to his feet. His ruined ankle screamed out in protest. He looked down; it had swollen to three times its normal size, and was poking outwards at an unnatural angle.

"I'm okay, kid, you can let me go."

The man released him and he slowly, painfully hobbled over to the other vehicle. The impact had spun the vehicle around so that it was facing in the opposite direction; crowds of people had begun to form around the car, chattering and mumbling between themselves.

Gunn shouted. "Let me through, I'm a police officer."

He continued slowly, pushing his way through the crowds of bystanders. He approached the smashed car, the entire driver side door had been damaged, and he looked at the woman inside. Her face was slick with fresh blood. She appeared to be breathing, but it seemed slow and laboured.

Gunn addressed two men from the crowd. "I'm DCI Mark Gunn from the Greater Manchester Police. I understand that the emergency services have been contacted. Can you stay with this woman until the ambulance arrives?"

The two men looked at each other with a puzzled look. "Well, yes, we can, but you're not meant to leave the scene of a crime. If you're the police, you should know that."

Gunn shouted at the man, spittle flying from his mouth. "I have to go; it's a matter of life and death.

Make sure you stay here with the woman. When the police arrive, let them know that I had to go and apprehend a suspect."

Turning from the men, he slowly began to hobble away. He continued down the footpath, painfully dragging his injured appendage behind him. In the distance, he heard the sounds of sirens approaching.

Ten minutes later, Gunn was just making his way into the industrial estate in Prestwick. His entire body dripped with sweat from exertion and pain. His breathing continued to be difficult as he struggled to take in large breaths of air; a strange rattling sound emanated from somewhere within his chest.

He continued hobbling, gritting his teeth with determination as he entered the estate, the dilapidated buildings lay back from the main access road, and the July sun continued to blaze down. The buildings cast long shadows down from the rooftops, and glass reflected bright light into his eyes, making him squint. The area was silent – totally deserted. It reminded him of the old films that he had seen of the Wild West. The irony wasn't lost on him.

He continued to limp along painfully, until he located the building in the distance that he was looking for. It was a single factory unit, which stood away from any other buildings. The main perimeter of the building was enveloped in dull, grey steel cladding. The sign hung above the main entrance – a large industrial door. To the right of the unit was a steel fence. Three of the fence panels were missing, leaving a small gap. Gunn made his way around the side of the building, carefully climbing through the small gap, avoiding the weeds that overgrew the underside of the fence. He followed the building around, attempting to keep his back against the wall until he reached the personnel door. Composing himself, he took a deep breath, his whole body screamed out in pain. Perspiration had totally soaked through his shirt, and sweat ran down from his forehead, and dripped from his nose.

Reaching out his right hand tentatively towards the door handle, he gave it a quick twist. To his surprise, it turned. He pushed the door forwards slowly with a creak, and carefully stepped into the room. Directly facing him was a small sales counter, it stood vacated. Behind the counter was another access door that led out into the main factory area.

Quickly flipping up the hatch on the counter, he made his way through the door and into the factory. Overhead, dim strip lights illuminated the vast space. It took a couple of seconds for his eyes to adjust to the darkness. In the distance, about thirty feet away, two car maintenance ramps were suspended in the air. They held two vehicles. Below the first ramp, he could make out the silhouette of a female tied to a chair, and below the second ramp sat a vacant seat.

Approaching slowly, he began to search around, trying to keep any potential movement within his peripheral vision. A few laboured steps later, and he could recognise the figure. Bound to the chair was Melissa. His pulse quickened as he identified her; she was an utter mess. Her hair was all over the place, clung together with sweat and blood, and her torso was filthy, plastered in a mixture of dirty water, various other bodily fluids and grime. As he got closer, he could see that someone had bound her face in filthy bandages, which were already soaked with fresh crimson liquid.

She spoke as he got closer. "Who's there?"

"Melissa, it's Mark," he began. "I've come to get you out."

"Oh my God, Mark, you have to –"

Gunn felt the explosion of pain in the back of his skull. He never got to hear the end of Melissa's statement as he fell to his knees, his body toppled forwards and his face hit the filthy concrete with a thud.

****

The first thing that Jessica felt, as she woke up, was the agony erupt like a volcano inside her cranium. She slowly opened her eyes, rolled over onto her back and stared at the ceiling. The room span, her vision was blurred; objects came in and out of focus.

Grabbing her mobile phone from her pocket, she checked the display: No missed calls. Searching through her recently dialled numbers, she found the number for DCI Gunn and hit the call button. The phone rang out, but nobody answered. After a few moments, it went to answerphone.

Shit, Gunn, what are you up to?

She pressed the button to disconnect the call, and slowly pulled herself to her feet. She walked over to where Charlie's corpse lay down on the carpet. She put a hand to her mouth and stifled back the tears.

She shook her head. *Why?*

She snapped back from her reverie as the mobile phone in her hand began to vibrate. The shrill sound of the ringtone filled the air. Looking at the phone, the display read, *Mark Gunn Calling.*

Pressing the button to accept the call, she snatched the phone to her ear. "Sir, you really need to tell me now, what the fuck is going on?"

A voice came from the other end of the line. "Hello?"

"Hello, Melissa, is that you?"

"Jess, is that you. It's Gunn. You need to –"

The line abruptly went dead.

Jessica looked at the display on her mobile. It stated that the call had been terminated. Frantically, she pressed the redial button. The phone cut straight to answerphone, without ringing. She tried again, exactly the same process.

He's turned off his phone. He doesn't want to be traced.

Desperately searching through her phone contacts, she found the number for Chief Constable Rollins, and hit dial. The call was answered after a few rings.

"Jess, what have you got for me?"

"A mess, sir. Charlie is dead. I need an ambulance and an evidence team at her house, straight away."

"What?" He snapped, "What the hell is going on? Where's Gunn?"

Jessica hesitated before responding. "Sir, I think Gunn is involved."

Four minutes later, Jessica heard the sirens of the ambulance as it pulled into the street; she went to the door and waved it down. Two medical operatives stepped out from inside the ambulance cabin, and approached.

The first man spoke. "Where is it?"

Jessica snapped. "*She* is back through there."

She stood aside as the two men entered the house. As she continued to stand in the driveway, she observed as a police car pulled up and parked behind the ambulance. The door opened and Jack Rollins jumped from the vehicle, looking extremely agitated.

He approached Jessica. As he drew near, he observed the large lump that had started to form on her forehead. "Jesus, what the hell happened to you?"

"I had an argument with a door frame. The door frame won."

"Gunn?"

"Yes, we had an argument, he threw me across

the room and disappeared."

"What was the argument over?"

"He found a note on Charlie's body. He read it and just flipped out. I tried to stop him, I even used pepper spray, but it didn't work. Sir, I'm not sure but I think he's connected to this in some way. When I finally came back around, I tried ringing him. I got no answer. Then I got a call back from his number a few seconds later. He has Melissa."

A look of worry began to spread over the man's face. He was becoming more agitated by the second. "Jess, I'm pulling you off this case."

"What? But, sir, if Gunn is involved then –"

"No, you're too close to the people involved. Half of your team are already dead, the other half are missing. I'm re-assigning another team. Jump in the car, I'll give you a lift home. You can fill me in on any relevant information on the way."

They continued to talk as they slowly filtered their way through the city centre traffic.

"What's the situation with Daniels?" She asked.

"He's in the hospital, under guard, he's still unconscious. Gunn made a right mess of him."

"Maybe that's why he was so insistent on trying to get him to confess?"

He looked at her. "Maybe you're right. I've got a bad feeling about this whole thing. Something just doesn't add up, at least at this point. We know that Melissa is alive, that's something, at least."

"Sir, that's another thing. We found a camera on Charlie's body. He's already started in on her. Whoever is doing this has cut her eyes out."

Taking his eyes from the road, he stared at her, incredulously. "What the fuck? What did Melissa say when you spoke to her?"

"She just said Gunn's name, and the line went dead."

"Is there anything else I should know?"

"When I went to the block of flats to search for further evidence, I found a pair of handcuffs. Sir, they were standard police issue."

He shook his head. "I really hope he isn't involved in this mess."

He pulled the car from the stream of traffic and into the car park of Jessica's apartment block. He pulled into a parking space, and yanked on the handbrake.

He turned to Jessica. "Listen, I want you to take a couple of days off. I don't want to see you anywhere near the station, I certainly don't want you turning up at any crime scenes, and you are off the case. Is that understood?"

"Yes, sir. Can you keep me informed if you learn anything new?"

"Just make sure that you can be contacted and I will speak to you in a few days."

"Okay, sir. Thanks."

She opened the car door and walked across the car park to the main entrance to her apartment block. As she walked past, she noticed that Alex's BMW was parked in its reserved space. She held the key fob up to the electronic device on the main door and it unlocked.

She walked up the main corridor to the front door of her apartment and unlocked the door. She entered the apartment and called out. No reply

"Hey, it's me."

As she entered the kitchen, she spotted Alex. "Hey, baby, I could murder a painkiller."

Alex turned around from inside the fridge and spotted her. "Hey, what the hell, happened to you?"

Alex approached and touched the bump on Jessica's head. "Ouch, that as painful as it looks?"

"Yep. And as of right now, I'm off the case."

"What? How come?"

"Rollins took me off it; he said that I was too

close, after everything that's been going on."

"To be honest, baby, I can't say that I'm not relieved."

"What?"

"It's getting dangerous, people are actually dying. I tell you what, I've got to head back into work this afternoon. Tonight, when I'm finished, let's go out for a meal, my treat."

Jessica smiled, and they passionately kissed. "You're on."

Killer's Got Their Gunn

I stand and watch as he sits there slouched to his left, unconscious, tied roughly to the chair. A sliver of blood runs from the back of the head, where I hit him with the wrench, and it's started to drip to the concrete floor from his ear.

I feel an excitement that I've never felt before. Even the euphoria that I felt when butchering those whores doesn't come close to this. This is what I've spent the last months preparing for. The meticulous planning and execution has all come down to this one defining moment; the capture of DCI Mark Gunn.

I check the equipment, check that everything else is in place. I'm going to enjoy this next part. Vengeance is mine, and it will be wrought. This man has been getting away with his filthy tricks and shady practices now, for way too long. It's time to make him pay. I want to see him beg for his life.

However, that's not before showing the whole world what a complete coward he is.

Checking the machinery controls and lifting equipment is set up and operational, I check the bonds that hold both of my captives to their chairs. They're going nowhere. I take a glance over at the woman, and I'm amazed that she has survived for this long. The bandages that cover her face are drenched with grime and blood. Judging by the smell of her, I think she's had an accident.

She has certainly been resilient, a tougher cookie than the detective here. I kick out viciously and my foot connects with the man's knee. A satisfying cracking sound echoes around the warehouse, and he begins to mumble. It looks like he's beginning to wake up.

Just in time, I have a game to play.

DCI Gunn slowly began to open his eyes; the pain erupted inside his head like a nuclear explosion. The sour, coppery taste of blood lined his throat, his chest continued to wheeze. With his blurred vision gradually coming into focus, he slowly inspected the surrounding area. His hands were fastened securely behind his back. Despite his frantic attempts to free them, they weren't going anywhere.

He looked to his right. Melissa sat in her own seat, her head lolled forwards. She was asleep, or most likely sedated.

He called out to her. "Melissa?"

No answer.

He looked around; and both of them were placed directly beneath the slant of a car maintenance ramp. As he looked up, he saw the underside of a car chassis hovering above him.

He called out again. "Melissa?"

From behind him, a voice spoke.

"She won't hear you just yet, DCI Gunn."

He attempted to turn round, but could not locate the voice. "What, who the fuck are you?"

He heard the sound of footsteps falling on the concrete behind him as the figure slowly emerged from the shadows and walked into view – a sudden spike of recognition.

He shook his head, and laughed. "You?"

"Me."

"So what's this all about?" he asked, "I've got people being tortured left all over the city."

"What if I was to tell you that it's about nothing?"

"What?"

"What if I simply enjoy creating carnage within this god forsaken cesspit of a city?"

"I wouldn't believe you."

"Ah, I see you're having one of those legendary DCI Gunn hunches again. It's those fucking hunches that got you in this situation in the first place."

He frowned. "How do you mean?"

"DCI Gunn, the detective who always gets his man, whether they are guilty or not. All of the women that I've killed have all been insignificant. If your hotshot officer Sinnamond would have used the one vital bit of information available to her, then you may have gotten to me before I got to you. It's been fun playing cat and mouse with you, but you really didn't have a clue, did you?"

Gunn shook his head. He thought back to each of the circumstances for the murders, furious with himself. Putting the pieces together in his mind, now, it all made perfect sense. He cursed himself for missing something so obvious.

"Hey, you never know, I might be feeling generous and let you go. Then maybe you can pin all of this on your man, Daniels, and I can disappear forever."

Gunn stared. "I somehow suspect that that's not very likely, is it?"

""You bet your fucking arse it's not very likely. You see, framing Daniel's is your style. Let's face it, it's not the first time that you've stitched up an innocent man."

Gunn frowned. "Is that what this is all about?"

"Tell me, Detective Chief Inspector, do you remember the name Matthew Rippin?"

The officer's heart sank at the mention of the man's name. He looked down to the floor. He didn't respond to the question.

"Answer me before I cut Melissa's throat. Do you remember the name Matthew Rippin?"

"Yes."

"Yes, what?"

"Yes, I remember Matthew Rippin."

"Good, then maybe you're beginning to understand why you've found yourself in these unfortunate circumstances."

Gunn spat, "Rippin was guilty."

"No, he fucking wasn't. You pinned those charges on him, and he was sent down. Whilst inside, he committed suicide. At least, that's what his family were told. He hung himself in his cell, a little too cliché for my liking."

Gunn hissed. "He got what was coming to him. He was a fucking nonce."

Like lightning, a gloved hand came from nowhere and connected with the officer's nose. The blow was hard enough to snap cartilage, his head thrown violently backwards. His head collapsed forwards and he spat a huge wad of saliva and blood onto the concrete floor in front of him.

Gunn stared, defeated; he knew he was a dead man. "So who are you?"

"Matthew Rippin was my older brother. When we were young, he looked after me. You framed him, caused his incarceration and ultimately, his death. He didn't commit suicide, he was murdered. Look around you, all of these murders, all of this blood is on your hands."

Gunn laughed. "You're a psychopath."

"Maybe I am, but so are you. The only difference is that I accept my identity; I don't use the media frenzy to give the public a false sense of security, to lie that their man has been caught, and use the attention to bolster my own delusions of grandeur. You are the most dangerous type of sociopath, and yet you carry a badge that makes everything you do legal."

Gunn noticed a red light appear to his left as a video camera turned on.
"What do you want from me?" He asked.

"That's quite simple; I'm going to give you a choice."

"A choice of what?"

"It's your life, or hers. Whatever choice you make will be honoured. You can either choose to die as a hero, or live like a coward."

Gunn looked over to Melissa, who had started to come back around.

"Ah, Melissa, I see you have woken up just in time."

Melissa grumbled. "What… what's going on?"

"DCI Gunn, above you both, on maintenance ramps, are two vehicles. In my left hand, I have the hydraulic control for Melissa's ramp, and in my right hand, I have the controls for yours. You have sixty seconds to make your decision, just tell me, left or right. Your time starts now."

Gunn frantically pulled against the restraints that held his hands. The plastic cut into his flesh and he started to bleed, but the binds didn't budge.

He looked over to Melissa, who still looked groggy.

"Melissa, can you move?"

She didn't respond.

A voice called out. "Forty seconds."

Sweat began to pour down Gunn's face as he panicked. His heart was thundering in his chest. He struggled again, to no avail.

He screamed. "Fuck you. I won't choose."

"Then you die, by default. Thirty seconds."

He looked over to the sorry sight of Melissa, the bandages covering her ruined face. Gunn thought back to the case against Rippin. The short cuts that he had used, the lack of evidence, the bribing of several eyewitnesses. He had seen paperwork from the prison, stating that Rippin's death was organised by the other prisoners.

"Twenty-five seconds."

Gunn panicked, and attempted to throw the chair forwards, but it had been secured to the ground. He frantically kicked out at nothing. Desperate.

"Twenty seconds, make your decision. Left or right."

Gunn looked over to Melissa, she was looking around, and she had no real idea about what was going on around her.

"Ten seconds."

Gunn turned and addressed his officer. "Melissa, I'm sorry."

"Five seconds."

Gunn screamed. "Left."

Melissa screamed.

Gunn looked above his head and screamed as the hydraulics in the maintenance ramp gave an audible gushing sound before the ramp came crashing down onto his head.

"DCI Mark Gunn. Selfish and gutless, right until the end."

Melissa span her head round. She pleaded. "So are you going to let me go?"

"I'm sorry Melissa, I can't be leaving any loose ends."

Melissa's scream cut short as the maintenance ramp came thundering down onto her.

Killer Got Their Gunn

Jessica and Alex sat in the restaurant opposite each other. They sat intently at the table as Jessica looked into Alex's eyes.

"You know, you really do have the most beautiful eyes."

"Thank you. Yours aren't so bad either."

"So, what are we going to order? What about a bottle of wine?"

"Never mind the wine, what about a bottle of Champagne?"

Jessica whistled. "Ooooo, Champagne, pushing the boat out, aren't we?"

"Perhaps you could say that. Today, I've managed to get something sorted, something that has been on my mind for a while."

"Sounds intriguing, what was it?"

"Never mind, just something at work that I had to take care of."

Jess smiled. "So, what's the plan for tonight then? I hope you're planning to wine, dine and sixty-nine."

They both laughed, and looked around the restaurant sheepishly. Luckily, nobody had paid any attention to the statement.

"So, Jess, tell me about the case, where are they up to with it?"

"You know I can't speak to you about the case."

Alex laughed. "It's never stopped you before. How close are they to actually catching this guy?"

"Well, the truth is that they don't really have anything to go on at all. None of the evidence has shown up any real leads. All of our enquiries have been dead ends, and this Daniels guy looks like a red herring."

"So, where is your boss? This Gunn guy?"

"Nobody knows. At the moment, he's being treated as a suspect, in connection with it all. The evidence against him is fairly circumstantial, but he was the last one to know the whereabouts of Melissa."

Alex grinned. "It looks like you're best kept away from him then, a man that lives his life like that shouldn't be surprised when his world comes … shall I say, crashing down on him."

"I think maybe you're right. This whole case has had me reconsidering whether this is actually what I want to do with my life."

"How do you mean?"

"Well, it's proven that I don't really have the stomach for this sort of thing. I'm thinking about leaving, or at very least getting transferred from the murder squad."

"I must admit, I can't say that I'm not relieved."

Suddenly, a waiter appeared at the table and asked if they were ready to order. They placed an order for their food, before Alex asked the waiter to deliver a bottle of Champagne.

Jessica winked at Alex. "With two glasses."

"I'm driving, just the one glass for me."

Jess leaned forward. "Leave the car here, and let's go into town and get fucked up. It's been ages since we've had a proper blow out. Let's go and get some pills and coke, and go clubbing. I'm off work for a few days, and you can take the day off tomorrow, let's go mad for once."

"Pills and coke? You do realise that you're a police officer?"

She winked. "That just means that we know the best places to get them from."

"Oh, well, if you insist, I know just the place that we could go."

"Where?"

Alex grabbed her handbag from the ground, beneath the table, and began rooting around inside. She pulled a book of matches from inside and threw them down on the table. Jessica picked them up and inspected the bright logo on the front of the pack.

"The Loft?" She asked.

The other girl giggled playfully. "Yeah, I've been there a number of times. Apparently, it's the place be seen."

Chief Constable Rollins walked through the main doors to the Manchester Police Headquarters. He was tired; the black rings around his eyes and the worry lines upon his brow, both evident. He was a man under extreme pressure. He walked through the main entrance corridor with his shoulders slumped, his head hanging low and his feet dragging along the floor. He scratched at the three-day-old greying stubble around his chin. The last few days had really taken its toll on the man.

It had been exactly two weeks since DCI Mark Gunn's disappearance. He assigned a new team the very same day; an external unit who flew up from London that evening. Briefed and informed, with the information that Rollins had spent the remainder of the day collating, they were ready.

Not the largest amount of information, but a start nonetheless.

Since the day that Gunn had disappeared, nothing new had turned up. No one discovered or reported any bodies within the city. After two days of total carnage, everything had gone suddenly quiet. The new team struggled to get any further along with their enquiries than Gunn's team had. They were hitting a dead end at every available lead.

Rollins was now facing mounting pressure from his own authorities for a result, or they were threatening to pull the funding and suspend the investigation. He owed it to the victims to find Gunn; he owed it to their families, to the public, to himself.

He continued the slow walk down the main corridor of the station and began the long ascent of the stairs that led to his office on the upper floors. Checking in on the office where the new investigation team had been working, he noticed that it was empty. No information had been left lying about; there were still various case photographs and notes hanging from the walls.

All out on enquiries.

He continued into his office and opened the lid to his laptop, the sound of the hard drive firing up whirled, and he clicked into the dialogue box that prompted him for his password. He entered the name of the first dog from his childhood and the obligatory number required to complete the field, and the desktop fired up before his eyes.

Clicking on the logo that opened up his mail server, he shook his head when he saw that he had forty-three unread messages. He could clearly see that the majority of those messages were from his two direct commanding officers. He sighed as he slowly started to click on the messages and read the content.

He jumped when there was an abrupt knock at his office door.

He minimised the message on his computer screen and turned to face the entrance to his office. "Come in."

The door slowly opened, and a young desk sergeant entered the room.

"Sorry to interrupt you, sir, but this package came for you in the post."

"Thank you."

The man handed over the brown Jiffy bag, turned, and exited the office. Chief Inspector Rollins touched the padded envelope, looked at it.

Addressed to him, and marked as strictly private and confidential. He was unsure of its contents, he wasn't expecting anything, but there was a postmark that it had been addressed from London.

Rollins pulled the envelope open and looked inside. There was a single, digital disc, and a hand written note that said two solitary words. *The Truth.*

He frowned, turned, and slid the disc into the compartment at the side of his laptop. After a few seconds, the media player on the device popped up onto the screen. It took him a few moments for his eyes to adjust to what he was seeing in the grainy, dark pixels on the display. When he realised what it was, his hand shot to his mouth in utter shock.

On the screen in front of him, he saw the image of DCI Mark Gunn, frantically thrashing about whilst bound to a steel chair. In the background, he could just make out the silhouette of what looked like Melissa. He fumbled, quickly turning up the speakers; there was a faint hissing noise before the voice of a woman blasted over the computer speakers.

"It's your life, or hers. Whatever choice you make will be honoured. You can either choose to die as a hero, or live like a coward."

Killer Got Her Gunn. And The Girl.

For more information about other work from these authors please go to:

http://matthickmanauthor.blogspot.co.uk/?m=1

or

www.andrewlennon.co.uk

Printed in Great Britain
by Amazon